An Errand for Emma

An Errand for Emma

Chad G. Daybell

ISBN: 1-55517-422-1

v.2

Published by: **Bonneville Books**
Distributed by:
925 North Main, Springville, UT 84663 • 801/489-4084

CFI
Publishing and Distribution Since 1986
Cedar Fort, Incorporated
CFI Distribution • CFI Books • Council Press • Bonneville Books

Cover design and page layout by Corinne A. Bischoff
Printed in the United States of America

To Tammy,
my wife and best friend.
Her inspired ideas and suggestions
made this book possible.

Chapter One

I tumbled down the Wilkinson Center stairs, bounced off a wall and rolled to a stop. I rubbed my bruised knees as one of my Brigham Young University classmates rushed to my side.

"Emma, that looked terrible!" he said. "Are you all right?"

"I think so. My knees took the worst of it." I gathered up my scattered textbooks, and he helped me to my feet.

"Wow! I was sure you'd crack your head open."

"I'm afraid this happens too often," I said. "I've had worse falls. My feet just do what they want sometimes."

"So you'll be OK?"

"I'll be fine. Sorry to scare you like that." I gave him a smile to show I'd survive, and he went on his way.

I sometimes grow weary of apologizing for such exploits, but I've learned to accept these gifted feet of mine—not that I'd wish them on anyone else. But if I weren't such a klutz, I never would've been sent on the journey that changed my life and the lives of my ancestors. So being clumsy has had some benefits.

My adventure began innocently last summer at my home in Springville as Mom and I waited for our visiting teachers to arrive. Beth and Leah Jensen are white-haired elderly siblings who live around the corner from us, and they've been our visiting teachers since I was three years old. Their visits always followed the same pattern, starting with a chat about the neighbors, then questions about how our family was doing. They usually closed the visit with an inspiring experience from their mission together to Florida. Then Leah would often say, "Emma, I believe your endless accidents have a deeper purpose, sort of a mission of your own. Just don't get yourself killed trying to complete that mission!"

That comment always bothered me. It seemed absurd to say

my clumsiness had a higher purpose. But I could shake off Leah's abrasiveness because she was my favorite of the sisters. Both are wonderful people, but Leah draws people to her like a magnet, while Beth often gets too bogged down by mundane tasks to let anyone get close to her. When I first read in the Bible about the sisters Mary and Martha who were Jesus's friends, I immediately thought of Leah and Beth. Leah is like Mary, who took the time to listen to the Master, while Beth lives as Martha did. She does necessary chores and church callings, but rarely devotes time to the Savior or to savoring spiritual things. When they taught classes at Springville High during their younger years, the students nicknamed them "The Fire and Ice Sisters." Leah fired up the students, but Beth never warmed up to anyone.

Leah had taken me under her wing over the years. We would sit together at church, and we'd work together planting flowers or raking leaves in her yard. It was during these times she became my own "Dear Abby." I'd ask her questions about life and the church, and she would share her opinions on the subjects. For example, when Mom and Dad told me I couldn't date until I was 16, I really resented it. But a 10-minute chat with Leah the next day helped it make sense. It was during one of those leaf-raking sessions that I asked Leah a question I'd been pondering.

"Leah, I've seen your family pictures on your wall. You were an attractive young woman. Didn't you ever have an opportunity to get married?"

She laughed and said, "I've only saved my most flattering pictures. I've suffered through plenty of bad-hair days." Then a sorrowful look came into her eyes. She leaned her rake against a tree and pointed down the street to a two-story house.

"Yes, I had my opportunity. As a teenager I went steady with Harold Milton, who lived in that house. We'd been childhood friends, but in high school a romance began to blossom between us." Her eyes twinkled at the memory. "We planned to marry after we graduated, but the attack on Pearl Harbor turned our world upside down. I feared Harold would have to go to war, and sure enough, he was drafted into the Army soon after graduation. He wanted us to get married before he went overseas, but I didn't want to rush into anything. I felt the Lord would watch over Harold and bring him safely home."

Leah paused and gave me a small, sad smile. "Let's go sit on the porch. I haven't told this story in a long time, and it's taking a lot out of me."

I took her arm, and we settled on the top step. "Both of our families urged us to get married, but I was only 18, the same age as you," she said. "I was so confused. Harold begged me to go to the Justice of the Peace with him that final night, but I refused once again, so he finally knelt before me and pulled out a ring.

"He said, 'Leah, please promise me you'll marry me the day I get home!' I agreed, and he slipped the ring on my finger. Two months later I found out that my soldier boy had been killed in Europe when a grenade landed in his foxhole."

I wrapped my arms around her as we fought back tears. Then Leah held up her left hand, and I noticed a plain silver band around her withered ring finger. "I've kept my promise to Harold, and I hope he keeps his part of the deal."

The Jensen sisters had always visited us on the third Tuesday of the month at 4 p.m., rain or shine. They didn't like to visit too early in the month, on the rare chance they'd miss some important news in our lives, but they also didn't want to procrastinate until the end of the month. So the third Tuesday worked for all of us.

So on July 20th at 4:10 p.m., Mom and I sat on our couch, surprised the Jensen sisters had missed their first appointment in nearly 200 months. We looked uneasily at each other as we heard sirens approaching our block, and a sense of foreboding settled on us. Then the phone rang, and I jumped up to answer it.

"Hello?" I could hear Beth crying on the other end of the line.

"Beth, talk to me. What's wrong?"

"Emma, we won't be visiting you today."

"What happened? We heard the sirens…"

"Leah has collapsed! I think she had a heart attack!"

"We'll be right there!" I slammed down the phone and rushed out the door with Mom right behind me. We ran around the corner and saw paramedics on the porch working feverishly to keep Leah alive, but their efforts soon slowed—then stopped completely. Mom went inside to comfort Beth, and I crumpled to the ground in tears, shocked to lose such a dear friend.

Beth later told us that as Leah shut their front door to leave for our visit, she slumped silently onto the porch. Beth hadn't been able to find a pulse, and by the time she finally returned to Leah's side after calling 911, Leah had likely reunited with friends and family in the heavenly courts above.

Chapter Two

Leah's funeral service was uplifting, but I had difficulty controlling my emotions. I had agreed to sing a vocal solo, but I couldn't stop crying during my rehearsal, so I took myself off the program. The talks were beautiful, but they kept me in tears, especially when Dad spoke of the impact Leah had made on our family. But by the time we drove from the church to the Springville Evergreen Cemetery for Leah's burial, I had settled into a somber, accepting mood.

I knew Leah would die someday, but this was too sudden. She'd been my anchor this past year as I'd lost—then slowly regained—my self-esteem. Our little family of four has always been very close, and life has gone smoothly for years. Dad is a well-respected electrician, and Mom is a full-time homemaker. They are nice, friendly people, but certainly not famous. As the oldest child, I felt sure I'd be the one to bring glory to my family. Doug was merely my messy younger brother who spent all his time playing sports and wouldn't amount to much.

Then last year Doug ruined my big plans. As a sophomore, Doug was named the starting third baseman on the Springville High baseball team. He did fine, but he wasn't a star. Then in the game to decide the region title, the Spanish Fork Dons had the bases loaded and one out in the final inning, with Springville ahead by a run. Spanish Fork's best player smashed a line drive down the third-base line, and it appeared the Dons were going to win. But Doug snagged the ball in the tip of his glove and quickly tagged the base runner. Double play! Springville had won the title!

A photographer caught Doug's catch on film, and The Daily Herald ran the photo across the top of its sports section with the headline "Dalton's defense defeats Dons." The sportswriter nicknamed him Doug "Double D" Dalton, and we've had a local celebrity in our home ever since. Doug's confidence soared, and he developed into Springville's best athlete. During his junior year, he was a star running back in football and then dazzled everyone as a basketball guard. Finally, he capped off this past baseball season by leading Springville to the state title.

Believe me, I'm not bragging. I just wanted to share why I've had a drop in self-confidence lately. It is undeniable that I'm athletically inferior to him. We have the same genes, yet he's so athletic, and I'm so clumsy. Thankfully, my parents do their best to not show favoritism. When there was an article in the newspaper about Doug, Mom made sure she also clipped out the honor roll and underlined my name in red ink before posting both clippings on the fridge. But she gave that up once she realized that Doug was in the paper at least once a week, while the honor roll came out only four times a year. Finally she just kept a scrapbook for Doug and hid it so I wouldn't feel bad.

I struggled a bit at becoming "Double D's big sister." His success wouldn't have bothered me so much, except that it never went to his head. If he'd been cocky, I could've still felt superior. But other than his not-so-hot grade point average, he's great! He's humble, handsome, and kind to everyone. Why did I have to be the flawed child?

I still hoped great things awaited for me, yet I had no idea what these things could be, compared to Doug's success. But when I was at my lowest, Leah was at her best.

"You seem a little down, dear," Leah would say. "Too many boys to choose from?"

"No, I just feel invisible at school and at home. It's always 'Doug this,' and 'Doug that.' I'm sick of it. There's more to life than Doug."

"You said it!" she replied curtly. I stared at her, glad she agreed. "Sports and popularity may seem important, but they don't mean much in the long run," she said. "Emma, you've got a mission to perform that will someday mean more than all of Doug's hits, touchdowns and baskets combined."

There was that "mission" talk again. Despite my own doubts about that mission, her assurances helped me keep my head up, even when the rest of the world thought I was just an airhead. My light brown hair, blue eyes and gangly frame did fit the mold, especially when combined with my clumsiness, but it just wasn't true. I did well in school and seminary, and I knew that somewhere there was a wonderful prince waiting for me who would understand his sometimes-spacey princess.

———

We arrived at the cemetery, and Dad pulled under the shade of two large trees. I got out of the car near a plaque that read, "Heritage Trees—Native Juniper Grove." Dad came around the car and looked at the plaque with me.

"This grove of juniper trees was here long before the original pioneers came," he said. "It was once a favorite campsite for the Ute Indians who lived in the area." He ran his hand along the rough bark of one of the trees. "Imagine the stories this tree could tell!"

Dad was one of the pallbearers, and he took his place near the hearse. Mom and I walked through the grove and stood near the gravesite. I looked at the many faces in the large crowd, both young and old. I suddenly realized what an impact this small, frail woman had made on so many lives besides just mine. Following the graveside service and dedicatory prayer, I approached Beth, who was sitting in a chair near the casket. I offered her my sympathies and gave her a hug.

"Please come visit me," she said. "I hope we can become better friends."

"I will, Beth. No one knows your flower garden better than me!"

We tried to smile, but our hearts were breaking. I gave her a kiss on the cheek. Then I removed a red rose from a flower arrangement and placed it on Leah's casket. I ran my finger along the casket's polished wooden lid. "Leah, thank you for everything you've taught me," I said softly. "I won't let you down."

As the crowd began to disperse, I walked over to my parents. I gave Dad a hug, and he said, "Emma, we are going back to the church to help with the luncheon. Do you want to come with us?"

"Oh, I think I'll just wander through the cemetery for a few minutes," I said. "I'll find a ride to the church." I watched them get into the car and drive away. Then I began a leisurely walk through the older part of the cemetery. I loved to read the dates on the headstones and imagine the lives these people had led. I noticed two stones side by side. One person had only lived a day, while the other had lived to be 103! It reminded me of one of Leah's favorite sayings: "All that matters is that we earn our eternal reward, since we all end up six feet under the ground." The memory brought tears to my eyes as I realized how true that statement was today. Leah wasn't known outside the city, except by former students, but she had earned her reward.

———

I walked down the slope, emerging from the cemetery's oldest sections and entering an area that was special to me, despite the lack of big headstones or ancient trees. I strolled over to the small brownish granite headstone where my great-grandpa Keith Dalton was buried. He had been killed in a logging accident many years ago, but stories of his courage while confined in a World War II prison camp were legendary.

His courage was likely inherited from Finity Dalton, who led his family from England to Utah in 1864. That pioneer family had loved horses and the outdoors, and those feelings had been passed down through the family line. Although I am more a bookworm than a rodeo queen, I always looked forward to the Dalton family parties, which were guaranteed to be loud, joke-filled and wonderful. There was always a strong unity there. You knew these people cared about you and would be there for you.

I bent down and brushed away some grass clippings from the face of the headstone. I wondered whether Grandpa Keith was satisfied with the direction of my life. After graduating from high school in May, I'd had a lot of extra time on my hands as I waited to start college at BYU in the fall. For the first few weeks of the summer, my friends Angie, Brandee and I celebrated our supposed "adulthood" by visiting the various dance clubs in Provo. I love to dance, partly because it is the only time

I'm surefooted. But country line dancing got too repetitious, and my friends rejected my suggestion to attend the church's Young Single Adult dances. They felt those dances weren't exciting enough, although I'd enjoyed them.

When we had started going to these dance clubs, I felt Mr. Right would emerge from the dark shadows and swirling strobe lights, sweep me off my feet and eventually take me to the temple. But my hopes were fading fast.

One Saturday night we found ourselves at a noisy Orem dance club. On this night, the dance beat was beginning to give me a pounding headache, and the closest thing to Mr. Right had been a guy named Andre. Andre's only flaws were that he was three inches shorter than I and he felt the need to slow dance no matter how fast the song's beat.

My friends noticed Andre's interest in me, and Brandee teasingly said, "I think someone really likes you!" We looked in Andre's direction and found him staring at me. He raised his eyebrows and smiled casually. I turned away, and Brandee said, "Go for it! He looks nice."

Andre quickly approached and asked me to dance a fourth time, so I decided to get to know him. I leaned toward his ear and shouted, "Andre, where do you work?"

"I'm in the process of switching jobs," he shouted back to be heard above the music. In other words, he probably got fired last week. This guy was really looking swell. I thought I'd test him a little and let him know where I was coming from, so I asked, "What do you do on weekends other than dance? Would you like to come to church with me tomorrow?"

"Oh, I haven't been to church in a while, but I'd like to go again soon. Why don't we go back to my apartment and discuss how to spend Sunday?" He pulled me tightly against him, and his hands slid from my back to my hips.

"Not so fast, jerk!" I immediately pushed him away and somehow resisted the urge to punch him in the face. "This isn't going to work, Andre! By the way, it's time you learn how to fast dance for a change!"

Andre reached out to grab my arm, but I gave him my

meanest glare, and he moved back into the crowd. I walked over to Angie. "That guy needs to learn some manners!"

Angie rolled her eyes. "Emma, you're too picky! Have a little fun!"

"I'd rather be too picky than not picky enough!" I was surprised Angie didn't support my feelings. "I'm going home!"

Angie had driven us there, and I knew neither she nor Brandee wanted to leave the dance, so I told them I'd take the bus home. I left the building and waited at the UTA bus stop for several minutes. Finally the bus arrived, and as I traveled home on that nearly empty bus, I cussed myself out. Why was I spending each Friday and Saturday night in this pointless routine? My friends seemed to be heading in a different direction than I wanted to go, and I was uncomfortable with their new thrill-seeking attitudes.

Fun and excitement were too high of a priority in their lives. Just six months ago we'd spent the night at Angie's house, discussing our hopes of marrying a worthy man in the temple for time and all eternity. Now my friends rarely mentioned church, and maybe I'd allowed my ideals to slip a little too. I admitted to myself that I hadn't seen any men at these dances who had temple marriage on their minds.

That was the last dance I attended with my friends. They invited me a few more times, but I never went, and the phone calls soon stopped. I realized I really didn't miss the dances, or my friends, either. We'd been inseparable in high school, but our time together had always centered around homework and school activities. Now, our mutual love of dancing wasn't enough to keep the bonds of friendship strong.

I now felt lonely—but liberated, ready to branch out and find new challenges! So my first challenging step into real life was to take a job at Springville's Hogi Yogi sandwich shop. Quite a big challenge, right? The job itself was a bit stressful as I tried to keep the customers happy, but when I finally received a paycheck I felt I was making progress in life.

I usually worked from noon to 8 p.m., so I had lots of free time in the morning—too much free time. I felt antsy. I did a few chores each day and even watched a soap opera for a week, but that just added to the tension. I could feel a void in my life, but how was I supposed to fill it?

———

One night as we were gathered around the table playing Scrabble and eating popcorn, I mentioned to Dad that I was feeling restless. He sat there thoughtfully for a moment, then went to the bookshelf and plopped a blue paperback book onto the table. I stared at the cover. "The Book of Mormon? Get real, Dad! I'm not that bored." Dad looked a little hurt, and I backpedaled a little. "I mean, I read it in ninth grade for seminary, and I didn't understand much of it."

"You've grown up a lot since then," he said. "I think you'll find it refreshing. It sure beats the plotlines of 'General Hospital.'" I had no argument there.

Doug had been listening to the conversation, and he said, "I'll be studying the Book of Mormon in seminary this year, so why don't I get a jump on the rest of the class? We all know I'll need any advantage I can get." He gave me a playful grin. "Let's have a reading contest, Emma. This one doesn't involve any type of coordination, so you've got a chance."

I picked up the book and nearly hurled it at him, but then we all started laughing. He'd won me over. I probably could've brushed off Dad, but I couldn't resist Doug's challenge.

"You've got a deal, little brother. If I win, you'll do the dishes for a month."

"And if I win, you have to go on a date with Billy!" The thought of dating his ape-like best friend was revolting, but it provided a strong incentive.

"It's a deal. Prepare to lose!"

It took a chapter or two to get used to the book's writing style, but by the time Nephi cut off Laban's head in the fourth chapter, I was hooked on the story. It would make a great movie, although all the violence would bring at least a PG-13 rating. Anyway, I figured it would take us a few months to read all the way through the Book of Mormon, but in just three weeks we were both nearly done. I had been reading it for up to an hour each day, and Doug fell way behind. But then he had to play in a baseball tournament in St. George, and he read nearly half of the book during the drive.

Dad questioned us every few days on what we'd been reading, just to make sure we weren't skipping pages. Doug enjoyed the wars and stories such as Ammon cutting off the arms of the Lamanites, while I found myself noticing themes, such as how nice guys don't always finish last. Time after time in the Book of Mormon the righteous prevail in the end, especially when Jesus visited America after His resurrection. I loved the way He treated the people and blessed them. It gave me hope that with a little perseverance and toeing the line, maybe someday the Savior will allow me in His kingdom, too.

As we neared the end of the book, Doug and I decided to finish together. We both were happy—he didn't have to do dishes, and I could avoid his pal Billy. We read the last two chapters as a family, and I could feel the Spirit strongly. For the first time in my life I began to understand what the gospel of Jesus Christ was about—helping families return to our Heavenly Father. I finally felt I had a testimony of the gospel—and just in time. I would rely on that testimony many times in the challenging months ahead.

As we finished reading, I closed my book and said, "The Book of Mormon is just one big family history album! Some of the family made it, and some didn't."

"That sounds a lot like our family," Dad said.

"What do you mean?" Doug asked. "Weren't all our ancestors members of the church?"

Dad laughed. "Sorry to burst your bubble, Doug, but your genes are a mix of royalty, average folks and downright scoundrels."

Doug and I stared at him in astonishment. We could understand the royalty part, but scoundrels?

Mom went to the main closet in our living room. "You two have never been very interested in our family history," she said. "I guess we'll have to reveal our family's darkest secrets to spark your interest!"

She brought out a hefty stack of books and folders and placed them on the floor in front of us. I'd heard Mom and Dad talk about these records before, but I'd been too caught up in school and other activities to really care.

"We have a lot of information on most of our family tree, but this Cooper family on my mom's side has been a real stickler," Mom said. "Mom was a convert to the church, and we hardly have any information. This line stops at my great-grandpa Thomas Cooper, Jr."

Well, if he's a junior, you know his dad is also named Thomas, don't you?" I asked.

"That's right. We even found Thomas Jr.'s parents and siblings living in Rhode Island in the 1850 U.S. Census," Mom said. "But all the census tells us is they were from England. Plus, Thomas Jr. vanishes around 1865. I have a suspicion he was in trouble with the law, and I wouldn't doubt he rotted away in a prison or got killed in a shootout."

That caught Doug's attention. "Cool! We've got our own Butch Cassidy!"

"Too bad he wasn't famous, because it would make the search easier," Dad said. "We've searched through many English records, but in 19th-century England the name Thomas Cooper was as common as Bill Smith is today. So finding the right Thomas has been like trying to find a slightly overweight friend wearing a hat and sunglasses at a BYU football game."

We all laughed, knowing he'd just described a good portion of the fans in Cougar Stadium on game day. "In other words, we've come across many guys that look like Thomas, but we'll never find him until we know his seat number."

"To be honest, it might take a miracle to ever find this information," Mom said. "I feel Grandpa and Grandma Cooper are busy in the spirit world teaching the gospel to our ancestors, preparing them to accept the ordinances of the temple. But their 'students' can't pass their 'final exams' and leave spirit prison for paradise until we find their records and do their temple work."

"Wow, I'd never even thought of that before," I said. "I figured our ancestors are just playing harps in the clouds until the Second Coming."

They laughed at me, but I wasn't joking. That conversation opened up my mind, and I spent a lot of time the following weeks reading through those records and getting to know the talented, spiritual, strange and psychotic ancestors who had preceded me, and who were thus a part of me. Also, the importance of temple work began to sink in. "Going to the temple" was no longer just the one Tuesday a month when Mom and Dad were gone for three hours. I now saw its purpose—to help those who had died without hearing the gospel make covenants with Heavenly Father and achieve eternal life!

My thoughts were interrupted by the noise of an approaching train on the tracks below the cemetery. I also saw an older gentleman start up a riding lawnmower off to my right. The funeral must be over! How long had I been standing there? I looked back toward Leah's gravesite and only a few people remained. If I were going to get a ride back to the church, I needed to start back quickly. But I took a moment and said a silent prayer.

"Heavenly Father, please open a way for us to find out about the Coopers," I prayed. "I know any tidbit of information, such as where they lived in England, will lead us to several more generations of my ancestors. Allow me to be an instrument in thy hands."

I closed the prayer, then began walking briskly back across the grass to the gravesite. The hot July sun was beating down, so I weaved my way around various headstones, trying to stay in the shade. I noticed a small gray headstone with a cute little lamb carved into its top, and I took a moment to inspect the stone more closely.

Honnnnnk, honnnnnk!

The blast of the train's horn startled me and sent me stumbling forward. I caught my toe in the grass and slammed headfirst into that cute lamb! I lay dazed, trying to think clearly over the roar of the approaching train. Then everything went dark as my head slipped from the headstone onto the ground.

Chapter Three

Gritty sand pressed into my cheek as I lay motionless on the ground. I felt movement near my head, and I opened my eyes to find myself staring into the face of a mouse that was pawing gently at my hair. I jerked my head up, and the mouse scurried away. Then I noticed the overpowering silence. I expected to hear the shrill train whistle that had startled me, or at least the whirring blades of the nearby lawnmower, but there wasn't a sound. Was I dead? No, I could feel the throbbing bump on my head where I'd crashed into the headstone, and I could taste sand on my lips.

I was surrounded by sagebrush, weeds and tall grass. This sure wasn't the Evergreen Cemetery. Or was it? I was in a grove of juniper trees, and in the distance to the east I could see Maple Mountain, as majestic as ever. I could see Utah Lake in the valley below, and the sun was still blazing down on me. This was the same scene I'd admired just moments before at Grandpa Keith's grave, but as I scanned the area for headstones or roads, there was no hint the ground had ever been disturbed. The landscape was as I'd always known it, just lacking modern developments. No cemetery, no railroad tracks, and no other human beings!

Could I possibly have knocked myself into a previous time? From the looks of things, maybe the Mormon pioneers hadn't even arrived in Utah Valley yet. Dad had mentioned the Indian tribes that inhabited this part of the valley before the pioneers arrived, and I knew they'd often sold their captives into slavery or tortured them mercilessly. Panic swept through me, and any curiosity was gone. I just wanted things back to normal.

"Hello, is anyone out there?" I shouted. "Please help me!"

Swoosh!

A hawk dived toward me from a nearby tree. Our eyes met

briefly as it decided whether I was worth attacking. Then it flapped its wings and streaked past me for a flight across the valley. My heart fluttered, and I crawled under the tree to gather my emotions. I kept telling myself that I must have given myself a concussion. Between this and Leah's funeral, my emotions were at a breaking point, and I began sobbing uncontrollably. This was insane!

I sobbed so long that my throat went dry. I realized I needed to find water soon or I'd suffer heatstroke. I wiped my eyes and looked down the slope where I knew a small stream ran. The stream's course was different, but it was still there.

I cautiously began walking through the trees to the stream when a man on horseback caught my eye. He was about a quarter-mile away on the other side of the stream, and he was riding at high speed. I could see his cowboy hat, and I ran in his direction.

"Mister, wait! Over here!" I really had no hope he would hear me, but he jerked his head in my direction. He scanned the hillside, but the horse never slowed down. I stopped in disappointment, knowing I'd never catch him, but my hopes soared as I looked where he was headed. I saw a small town about a mile to the north! Smoke curled slowly out of several chimneys. Civilization! I was still feeling stressed out and confused, but the sight of something familiar calmed me. I did a little dance of joy and began walking toward the town.

Thankfully I had worn sandals to Leah's funeral, because high heels would've been horrendous in that sandy soil. But my denim jumper didn't offer much protection against the sagebrush and prickly weeds. My arms and legs were quickly covered with scratches, and the terrain was so rough and overgrown I soon abandoned walking straight to town and returned to my original plan of getting a drink in the stream. Then I'd search for the road the rider had used.

The stream was only four feet across, but the bank was a complete mudhole. Then I noticed a dead tree limb sticking out into the water. I carefully walked to the end of the limb and began scooping several handfuls of cool water into my mouth. Feeling refreshed, I prepared to leap to the other side, but the limb shifted under my feet, causing me to bellyflop into the stinking black mud on the opposite bank!

I had a tough time extracting myself from the several inches of slime that oozed over me, but I finally got to my feet and sloshed to solid ground, spitting again and again to get the putrid taste out of my mouth. I had no way to wash myself off without making a bigger mess, so I let out a frustrated moan, wiped my hands on clumps of grass and searched for the road. I wandered for at least an hour, but there wasn't a trail in sight. I must've gotten turned around. I was getting very hungry and thirsty, and the afternoon heat had turned me into a dried mudpie. I sunk to the ground and began peeling dried mud from my arms.

Then it dawned on me that Heavenly Father understood my strange situation, even if I didn't. I bowed my head and pleaded, "Father, I don't know what has happened to me, but I ask for thy guidance and protection. Please help me find someone who can safely guide me through this mess."

I closed the prayer, waiting for some type of answer. A soothing feeling soon came over me, and I felt confident that my prayer had been heard. I sat there surrounded by weeds, pondering what to do, when I heard the faint galloping of several horses. I jumped to my feet, and through the weeds to the south I could see two wagons coming my way. They would pass about 100 yards to my right. I ran in that direction but stumbled several times, and it seemed certain they would pass me. The clatter of the horse's hooves grew louder.

"Come on, legs, you can do it!" I shouted, and my legs took on new life. I leaped around rocks and weeds, closing the gap between me and the wagons. I shouted frantically, but the men on the first wagon didn't hear me, and they quickly passed by. I had only one more chance. As the last wagon approached, I made one final leap, soaring through the tall weeds and sprawling across a dirt road into the wagon's path.

The wagon's driver yanked back on the horses' reins with all his might, yelling, "Whoa, Duster! Slow down, Nellie!" I cowered on the ground as the horses jerked to a stop two feet from my head. Their hooves stomped wildly in confusion, and dust swirled everywhere. The driver leaped from the wagon and grabbed the horses' bridles, probably saving my life. The wagon's other passenger, an older man, hastily dismounted and grabbed me under the arms, pulling me to safety at the edge of the road.

By now, the first wagon had stopped. Their worried shouts reached our ears. "What's going on?" yelled the other men. "Did you see a rattlesnake? Are the horses all right?"

"Brethren, stay with your wagon," the older man called back. "We've startled a precious young creature, but we'll be rolling again shortly." Then he turned to the young blond driver. "Whew, that was a close one. Nicely done, Jake."

Jake nodded. "Thanks. The horses seem fine. How is she doing?"

The man turned to me. He was likely in his 60s, but he was muscular, with a long gray beard and twinkling ice-blue eyes. My heart was still racing as he adjusted his suspenders and hat, then bent down and extended his hand.

"We gave each other quite a scare, didn't we?" he said with a concerned smile. "I don't believe we've been properly introduced, my young friend. I'm President Brigham Young."

Chapter Four

I took President Young's hand and got to my feet. I tried to not stare, but the dozens of paintings and photographs I'd seen of him failed to convey the powerful presence of the warm, friendly man standing before me.

"What's your name, young lady?"

"Brigham Young?"

"Uh, yes, that's my name..."

I blushed, then squeaked, "I'm Emma Dalton." The confidence I'd felt after my prayer had evaporated. In my flustered state, I had no way to explain to a prophet of God why I had suddenly sprawled across his path, but President Young treated me with gentle kindness.

"You have quite a bad bump on your forehead," he said. "Plus, it appears you strolled through a mudhole. Let us help you."

"Thank you. I'm very confused about everything."

Brigham helped me into the wagon seat, and I sat between the two men as we started rolling again. I could tell they were a bit curious about me, but neither spoke for a couple minutes until Brigham broke the silence.

"We are traveling to Springville to meet with Bishop Johnson and the Saints there," Brigham said. "I'm sure Sister Johnson will be able to doctor up that bump. I also hope we can find you a wash basin and some clean clothes."

"Oh yes, please take me into Springville," I said unthinkingly. "That's where I grew up." That brought surprised looks from the men, and I braced for their questions, but the first one took a different turn than I'd expected.

"Your last name is Dalton?" Brigham asked. "Several Daltons have joined the church. One family I remember well came to speak with me in Salt Lake a few years ago, and I felt impressed they should settle near Heber. The father's name is Finity. Are you related to him?"

Finity Dalton! The first Dalton in my family line to leave England for Zion! "Yes, we're related," I said cautiously, "although we've never met."

Our conversation halted as we passed a tannery that stunk horribly. I plugged my nose, but the odor still made my eyes water. That place certainly wasn't around during my day. I soon realized we were traveling along what would eventually become Springville's Main Street. We approached what is now 400 South and Main Street, and I noticed we would soon pass through a thick eight-foot-high wall made of dried mud that stretched for blocks.

"When did they build this wall?" I asked. "This must've taken months to build!"

"Where did you say you're from?" Brigham asked. I met his eyes but stayed silent. He watched me thoughtfully, then continued.

"This wall has been here for nearly 15 years," he said. "I instructed the leaders of each settlement to build walls around their towns in the early 1850s when the Indians were really bothering us. I think it has helped keep the peace."

I noticed the large wooden gates. "Do you shut the gates each night?"

Jake gave me a funny look. "You must've hit your head pretty hard," he said. "You act like you just got here from Europe!"

Brigham waved his hand at Jake, silencing him. "We still close them in this part of the valley because we've had some trouble around here lately. There was a battle up the canyon at Little Diamond two summers ago, and men from both sides were killed. Bad feelings still linger even now, but when the Indians come in peace, we gladly share our food."

"Yeah, every winter a group of Indians set up camp in that juniper grove we just passed," Jake said. "Their young braves like to harass people traveling this road." That sent a chill up my spine! I noticed the guns resting behind the seat and realized he was serious. Thank goodness it was summer when I ended up in that grove.

People began streaming out of the gate, shouting "Hello, President!" and waving excitedly. Brigham took off his hat and used it to wave to people. He knew many of the people by name and he'd holler out to them, asking how their crops were doing, if they'd built their barn yet, and so on.

We passed through the city gate and were greeted resoundingly by the "Boom-bah, boom-bah, boom-bah!" of a bass drum. The drummer stepped into the street ahead of us, leading a brass band. The band struck up a rousing tune, and we became part of an impromptu parade. I suppose the rider I'd seen earlier had let the residents know President Young would soon arrive. I leaned over to Jake. "Is this how it is in every town?"

"If they know we're coming, we always get a grand greeting," he said. "Everyone loves President Young, and he loves to visit with the Saints. He visits most towns only once or twice a year, if at all, so his arrival always creates a holiday."

I had traveled down Springville's Main Street a thousand times, but it had never enchanted me as it did this day. The narrow dirt road we had traveled on widened into a wide dusty street. There were no sidewalks or street lights, and the hard-packed dirt road had unfamiliar buildings along each side, but I knew it was home! Those were the same mountains towering above us. I smiled when we passed the future location of Hogi Yogi. A small farmhouse and corral occupied the site. I wouldn't be working tonight!

I watched in wonder as dozens of little children joined the parade, walking and skipping alongside the wagon, some with shoes, some barefooted. Jake slowed the wagon to a crawl, and some of the children handed Brigham handfuls of wildflowers or polished rocks. When his hands were full, Brigham handed the items to me.

"I want each child who greets me to feel my love for them," he said. "I hope as they grow up they'll remember times like these when they are deciding for themselves if this gospel is of God. And believe me, Emma, this work is of God." He stuck a few more rocks in my hand, then turned back to greet more children.

I enjoyed watching Brigham work the crowd. Even with the children demanding his attention, he made eye contact with as many adults as he could. He knew this was a big day for them, too. These people had sacrificed nearly everything for the gospel, and seeing the prophet meant a great deal to them. Receiving a wave or greeting from him meant even more.

I couldn't help but notice the residents' clothes. Despite the hot day, the men all wore plain wool pants, long-sleeve shirts and sturdy boots. Hats and suspenders were common, as were mustaches and beards. The women all wore long dresses, some more fancy than others, but none more fancy than the plainest dress in a modern closet. Sturdy boots or sandals were the ladies' favorite footwear. Most of the older women wore white bonnets, while most of the girls my age and younger wore their hair in braids.

After we passed by, the people would step into the road behind the wagon and follow us, and soon there was a pleasant mix of music, laughter and chatter. As we moved along, I noticed one little girl with blue eyes and light brown hair trying to keep up with us. She wore only a ragged gray dress and no shoes. She held a small piece of paper, and every few moments she would try to dart between the other children to reach the prophet, but her path kept getting blocked. Her mother followed closely behind and would encourage her to try again, but after the sixth or seventh try, both mother and daughter were near tears.

I tapped Brigham's knee and pointed to the girl. "That little girl has tried desperately to reach you," I said. "Please let her greet you."

Brigham caught sight of her, then he told Jake to stop the wagon. Brigham stepped off into the road and said, "I need a hug from that sweet girl in the gray dress."

The mother and daughter looked at each other excitedly. The crowd parted, and the girl ran on her tippy-toes to the prophet. Brigham swept her up in his arms, and she planted a wet kiss on his cheek. Then she timidly said, "I made this for you." She handed him the paper, which contained the words "I luv U." Brigham thanked her, gave her a hug, then sent her scurrying back to her mother. As Brigham got back on the wagon, I wiped my misty eyes and reached out to put the paper with the other gifts he'd received. He began to hand me the paper, but then pulled it back and put it in his shirt pocket. "I'll hang on to this one," he said.

We passed a new two-story meetinghouse on the corner of Center and Main streets, where I was accustomed to seeing the city's fire station. Then we crossed Hobble Creek over a sturdy wooden bridge before arriving at Bishop Aaron Johnson's large home on the northeast corner of 100 North and Main Street. The emotion of the parade died down, and most of the people in town crowded around Bishop Johnson's home. I was still in awe at what I was experiencing, but I calmed down enough to try figuring out what year it was. I knew Springville had been founded in 1850, and it looked like it had been around for several years. And I vaguely remembered that Brigham Young had died in 1877. Brigham was looking older, but he was nowhere near death.

He had also said that Finity had been living near Heber for "a few years." I remembered that Finity had arrived in the Salt Lake Valley in 1864. So I had probably dropped into the late 1860s! The Evergreen Cemetery, where I'd hit my head, wouldn't be created for more than 20 years! Things could've certainly been worse, but I felt depressed at the thought of life without cars, telephones, or TVs. As I got off the wagon, I realized something else was missing—indoor plumbing!

I slipped through the crowd and asked a group of teenagers on the porch where the restroom was. One girl said, "Restroom? What's she talking about?" The others gave me confused looks, but as I danced from one leg to the other, they pointed to a brightly colored outhouse near the barn. I rushed in, closed the latch and held my breath as much as possible. As I sat there, I found a slightly weathered copy of *The Deseret News*. The date on the newspaper's banner was July 15, 1868. Whew! Now I wouldn't have to make a fool of myself by asking which year it was. As I finished, I realized the paper wasn't in the outhouse just for casual reading. Oh, how I wished for a single roll of modern toilet paper!

I emerged from the outhouse and moved back through the crowd just as the prophet climbed onto a wagon to address the group. "Hello, wonderful Saints of Springville!" Brigham called out. "Thank you for the rousing welcome! We had an uplifting meeting this morning with the Saints in Spanish Fork, and I wish to speak with you tonight in the meetinghouse at seven o'clock. See you there!"

Brigham got down off the wagon and began greeting those who gathered around him. I stood back, waiting for Brigham to notice me. He began moving in my direction and I waved to him when he looked my way. He called out, "Emma, Sister Johnson is waiting for you in the house!" Then he was engulfed again by the crowd. I walked to the porch, where I was met by a smiling middle-aged lady. "Come in, dear," she said. "I understand you've had a long day. I am Sister Johnson, but please call me Rachel."

Rachel led me into a spacious kitchen filled with delicious aromas. "Please take a seat at the table," she said. "You can eat while I take a look at the bump on your head." She went to the kitchen's small fireplace and lifted the lid off a pot hanging over a low flame. She scooped out a heaping bowl of beef stew and placed it before me, then brought a big chunk of warm homemade bread dripping with butter and a glass of cool spring water.

"This is delicious," I said.

"President Young said you'd be hungry," she said. "Eat as much as you'd like."

I ravenously ate what was before me, and Rachel wasted no time in refilling my bowl. As I worked on my second helping of stew, Rachel stood before me and gently touched my forehead. "That's quite a bruise," she said. "How did this ever happen?"

"I tripped and hit my head on a rock."

"It looks like the rock won the battle, but you should be fine." She dipped a cloth into a bowl of water and cleaned the injury. "Your clothing has really taken a beating. Why don't you change into one of my dresses?"

She went into another room and brought back a pleasant-looking dress, complete with petticoats. I looked down at myself and saw that my shirt was hopelessly mud-stained, and my jumper was no longer denim blue. It was now denim black.

"Thank you," I said. "I'm really a mess, aren't I?"

Rachel smiled, then pointed the way to a bedroom. "I've filled a washbasin in there if you'd like to clean up."

I gratefully took the dress from her, entered the bedroom, and shut the door latch. I slipped out of my grimy clothes, took a cloth and dipped it into the washbasin. I wiped the cloth along the base of my neck, and I was astonished at all the dirt that came off. I again soaked the cloth and washed my face. The cloth again turned black with grime! Why hadn't anyone told me how muddy I was! These people surely thought I was a savage. I brushed through my hair and got the mud out of it, but I really could've used a shower.

The dress I'd been given seemed a bit heavy, especially for a July afternoon, but it felt comfortable. Then I slipped my sandals back on and looked around the room. The furnishings were modest, with just the washbasin, a chest of drawers and a bedframe holding a straw-filled mattress. The sight of that bed made me feel exhausted. I opened the door, and Rachel turned to look at me from the table where she was kneading bread dough. "Oh, Emma, that dress fits you well," she said. "And your face looks much cleaner!"

"It feels cleaner!" I said. "I fell into a stream this afternoon, but I couldn't rinse myself off very well. Thank you for your kindness." I looked longingly back into the bedroom. "Rachel? I was wondering if I could take a little nap on the bed. I feel very tired."

"That would be fine, I suppose. Let me gather your dirty clothing, and I'll try to clean them tonight." She then said, "The family will be going to listen to President Young's message at the meetinghouse within the hour. Would you like to go with us?"

"I'd love to, but I'm afraid I'd fall asleep during the sermon unless I take a nap."

She laughed. "Haven't you ever heard a sermon by President Young?" I shook my head. "Not even the most drowsy person can sleep during his talks. It's like listening to thunder!"

She could see I was nearly asleep on my feet, though, so she motioned me to the bedroom. "You need a rest," she said. "I'll wake you in a few minutes."

I lay down on the mattress. It seemed comfortable enough, and the down-filled pillow seemed heavenly against my face. I pulled a rough-textured blanket over me and quickly drifted off to sleep. It was a deep sleep, but it certainly wasn't very restful. My dreams were filled with jumbled, strange images. I soon felt Rachel gently shake me several times to wake me for the meeting, but I just couldn't open my eyes. She finally said, "Just keep sleeping, my dear. We'll see you after the meeting."

Then the strange dreams rolled on. In one dream my family was frantically searching all over Springville for me. In the following dream, I was stuck in that muddy stream again. Leah Jensen was on the bank saying, "You can't get out until you finish your mission!"

Then I found myself sucked down into the mud, buried in darkness. In the distance, I saw the words "Cooper" and "Denver" brightly illuminated—the only lights in the black void. The words began moving toward me, and soon they danced around my head, changing colors and growing larger. Then they began spinning, like helicopter blades, and I worried they would injure me. I ducked twice to avoid getting hit, but then the words' rotations coincided, and I knew I was going to get sliced in half. As the words swung toward me again, I let out a scream of terror!

Chapter Five

I awoke in a darkened room, cowering in fear, but I quickly realized it had just been a crazy series of nightmares! Whew, it was nice to be nestled in my bed. I vaguely remembered a dream about Brigham Young and traveling to Springville. Then came those crazy dreams about my family, Leah Jensen, and those spinning words. Just then the door slid open, and a lady stuck her head into the room.

"Emma, what's wrong?" she said. "We heard you cry out." It was Rachel! I really was trapped in 1868! I regained my composure and said, "I'm fine. I just had a terrible dream."

"That's understandable. You've had a rough day," she said. "But if you feel up to it, President Young and Bishop Johnson would like to speak with you."

I jumped off the bed, quickly fussed with my hair, then walked with her to the front room. As we entered the room, Brigham stood. "You're looking much better, Emma. How does your head feel?"

"It doesn't hurt anymore. Rachel took good care of me."

The sun was setting, and we paused as Rachel went around the room lighting a few candles. Brigham thanked her, then said, "Emma, I'd like to introduce you to Bishop Aaron Johnson. He's been Springville's leading citizen ever since he set up camp on the banks of Hobble Creek in 1850."

Aaron stood and shook my hand. I knew Aaron had been a close associate of Joseph Smith in Nauvoo, having served as Nauvoo's Justice of the Peace for several years. So I was a bit intimidated to be talking with such highly esteemed men.

"Very nice to meet you," I said. I turned back to Brigham. "I must apologize for missing the meeting. I just couldn't wake up!"

Don't worry," Brigham said. "I have a feeling that you might teach us more tonight than I could've taught you." He motioned for me to sit in a chair across from him, while Rachel sat next to her husband on a sofa. Once we were seated, Brigham said, "The Lord has granted me an occasional glimpse of what the future holds for the Saints, and during such glimpses, I have seen these valleys bustling with millions of people. There are temples dotting the valleys, but the world is in a terrible commotion."

Then he paused, looking at me closely with those gentle but piercing eyes. "And in the future there are no longer walls around these cities! You asked me some peculiar questions today for a person who has supposedly grown up in Springville."

I shifted nervously. "I'm from Springville, but this isn't how I remember it."

Brigham nodded. "I have prayed concerning your peculiar arrival among us, and the Lord has confirmed that you have come to us from a future time. Is that true?"

I let out a sigh of relief, glad that someone finally seemed to understand my plight. I nodded and said, "Yes, that's right."

Rachel gasped, but Brigham and Aaron nodded to each other. They'd obviously discussed me. Aaron knew every person who had ever lived in Springville, and he'd never seen me before.

"Go on, Emma," Aaron said. "We'd like to hear how you arrived here."

"I went to a funeral this morning at a cemetery located in that juniper grove south of town," I said. "At the cemetery I tripped and hit my head on a headstone. It knocked me out, and when I woke up I found myself in the same place, but in a different time. I saw a man riding a horse on the road below me, so I walked in that direction and eventually jumped in front of President Young's wagon. Now here I am! I've traveled more than 130 years back in time."

They all looked at me in astonishment, but they seemed to believe me, so I said, "Where I live, I mean, when I live is a great time to be a member of the church. I was raised in Springville, which in my day has a population of more than 18,000 people. Provo has nearly 100,000 residents, and BYU is well-respected around the world."

"What is BYU?" Brigham asked. I couldn't help laughing. I said, "I guess you haven't founded it yet. BYU stands for Brigham Young University, and more than 27,000 students attend school there. In fact, I plan to enroll there this fall."

"Hmmm, a university in Provo," Brigham said. "I'll have to ponder that idea."

I suddenly felt I'd said too much, but Aaron was perched on the edge of the sofa. He said, "I feel what you say is true, despite how impossible it seems. Could you tell us more about the church in your time? Is it prospering?"

I told them that the church had wards in nearly every nation, with nearly 60,000 missionaries preaching the gospel. "How is that possible?" Aaron asked. "Are half the men in the church on missions?"

"No, the missionaries are mainly young single men," I said. "Church membership is now at more than 11 million members."

That sent them rocking back in their seats. "Amazing!" Rachel exclaimed. "Who would've dreamed of such numbers?"

To further convince them, I added that it's well-known in my day that the Salt Lake Temple was built with empty shafts and holes in the granite walls for a future purpose. I explained how elevators and electric lights have been added to the temple. Brigham nodded. "That's right," he said. "The design has spaces for future uses. The walls are now only a few feet above the ground, but someday we'll complete it!"

"You will," I said. "It's a magnificent building, and in my day it's recognized throughout the world as a symbol of the faithfulness of the Saints."

"That's wonderful news," Aaron said. They slipped into silence—all this information was taking time for them to digest. Brigham put his hand to his chin and stared out the window. The silence was deafening to me, and I nearly babbled on when Brigham said, "I feel your journey here involves temple work, but why? We don't even have a finished temple. If we hadn't been driven from Nauvoo and our beloved temple there, things would be different. But it is in your day, not ours, that temple work will blossom into magnificent splendor."

"I feel the same way," I said. "There must be information about my ancestors here that has been lost or destroyed in my day." I then told them about the glowing words I'd seen.

"'Cooper' obviously refers to my mother's family," I said, "but 'Denver' doesn't make any sense. None of my ancestors lived there."

"But that's where you'll find your answer," Brigham said. "Your purpose will become clear as you travel there."

"To Denver? How long will that take?" I asked. "In my time, we can reach Denver in less than a day. How long does it take a train to get there?"

They broke into laughter. "Wait for a year or two. Then you can take the train," Aaron said. "Right now we lack both the train and the tracks. A trip to Denver takes four weeks on horseback and even longer with a wagon. Walking is the only other way."

A gloom settled on the room. Then Brigham's face lit up. "I feel the solution depends on your relative Finity Dalton. He will somehow help you reach Denver. Aaron, would you be able to spare two of your sons for a few days to guide Emma to Heber?"

"Of course, President."

"Very good. Emma, I'll write a letter you can give to Finity. I'll make it clear I expect him to help you in any way he can. But we shouldn't tell him, or anyone else, about your journey through time. Aaron and Rachel have heard me speak privately about the upcoming century, and I know they won't tell anyone what they've heard tonight. But most of the Saints aren't ready for such talk. It would be best to keep a low profile and not mention the future. Agreed?"

"Yes, President," I said. "You've all been so helpful. I'm grateful we crossed paths."

He smiled kindly. "Once you leaped in front of my wagon, I didn't have much choice in the matter, did I?"

Everyone was up by sunrise as we prepared to travel to Provo. It was July 24th, and 21 years earlier on this day Brigham had looked across the Salt Lake Valley and proclaimed, "This is the right place." A big picnic celebration was planned in Provo, and several Springville families, including the Johnsons, would make the trip. From there, two of Bishop Johnson's sons would lead me on horseback through Provo Canyon to the Dalton farm.

I had stayed up late with Rachel cleaning my clothes, and it felt good to wear them again. I put my hair in ponytails, then climbed into the back of the Johnsons' wagon. We departed at sunrise, passing through Springville's northern gate and working our way along what is now known as Ironton Hill. By late morning we turned west onto Provo's Center Street, where another brass band and the usual pomp greeted the prophet. I could see a great city forming as I looked at the two-story brick buildings that were sprouting up in a row. The wagon traffic was surprisingly heavy, although I'm sure President Young's visit caused most of it.

Our bumpy four-hour ride ended at what is now Pioneer Park on 500 West. Once the wagon stopped, everyone scampered off to greet friends, leaving me alone. I didn't mind, and I joined a crowd watching the brass band play. A few fiddle players and a washboard player had joined them, along with an older white-haired man holding a glass jug. The band launched into an extremely upbeat version of "The Spirit of God," and I clapped along, chuckling at the man playing the jug. He puffed with all his might, trying to keep up with the band's tempo. The jug's low "Hoot! Hoot! Hoot!" added a nice bass sound for a few minutes until the old man comically fell to the ground, visibly worn out. The crowd laughed and cheered, and he stood and bowed solemnly before grabbing his jug and rejoining the band.

I noticed Brigham standing near the park's stage talking animatedly with a tall, dark-haired young man. I hated to interrupt, but I wanted to say good-bye to Brigham before I left with the Johnson boys. I walked up behind him and gently tapped his shoulder. He looked back in surprise, then he broke into a wide grin. "Hello, dear sister! Are you about to leave?"

"Yes, but I wanted to thank you again for the help you've given me."

"It has been a pleasure. Let me introduce you to this young man. Joseph F., I'd like you to meet Miss Emma Dalton, a visitor from Springville."

The man took off his stovepipe hat and kindly shook my hand. "Nice to meet you," he said. "I'm Joseph Smith, or Joseph F., as they call me around here."

"Joseph F. was set apart as a member of the Quorum of the Twelve last year at the ripe old age of 28, "Brigham said. "He's so talented the Lord called him to be one of my counselors, besides being on the Provo City Council. He's an amazing young man with great things ahead of him."

Joseph stammered in embarrassment at that. Brigham gave me a wink and said, "He's still a young pup, though, still learning how to run things. But it's nice to know the church will be in good hands long after I'm gone."

Then Brigham changed the subject. "Joseph F., didn't you run into Finity Dalton during your mission to England?"

"I sure did," Joseph said, glad to talk about anything but himself. "He had joined the church years ago, but they'd never come to Zion. We convinced him it was time to come."

"Emma is leaving today to visit Finity and his family near Heber."

"Really? Be sure to tell him hello from me, and tell Mary I miss her cooking." He poked a finger at his skinny frame. "She helped keep a little meat on these bones while I was in England."

We chuckled, then a bugle sounded. "That's my signal," Joseph said. "It's time to get the celebration started." He shook my hand again, then climbed onto the stage.

"He has turned into a fine young man," Brigham said to me. "He's as fearless and faithful as his father Hyrum and uncle Joseph were, which is what we need right now." He glanced toward the stage. "Well, I better get up there."

I quickly stepped in front of him and gave him a hug. "I need to get started on my journey," I said. "Thanks for believing me."

"You're very welcome," he said. "But don't leave without this." He pulled a letter out of his jacket and gave it to me. "Once Finity reads this, I'm sure he'll help you in every way. Good luck! It has been a pleasure to meet you."

He started toward the stage, then turned back. "By the way, what do the people of the United States in your day think of old Brigham?"

"They say you did an amazing job leading the Saints to the West," I said. "There's even a statue of you in the Rotunda of the U.S. Capitol."

Brigham's eyes widened. "That's a surprise! Does my statue have horns on my head and a long devilish tail?" He grinned, then touched my shoulder. "Have a safe trip."

He turned and climbed onto the stage as Joseph began the ceremonies. Dozens of Saints now crowded around me, and I worked my way through them toward the street. But I took one last look at Brigham and Joseph, two prophets of the Lord—one currently leading the church, and one who was foreordained to someday do so. I thanked the Lord for allowing me to feel the power of Brigham's leadership skills and his closeness to the Spirit. He was an inspired man, and without him to point me in the right direction, I would've failed in the mission that lay before me.

Chapter Six

The Johnson boys were waiting for me along Center Street, and I waved to catch their attention. I had met 18-year-old Will and 8-year-old Moses that morning, and they would be good company. I'd been surprised to learn Moses was only eight because he handled himself like a small adult, but as sons of Bishop Johnson, they were accustomed to being asked to fulfill heavy tasks with little notice.

Rachel gave us sandwiches and loaded our supply bags. Then we were off! Will rode one horse and carried our supplies, while I rode behind Moses on the other horse. Will said that even at a steady trot we wouldn't make it to Heber by sundown, so we'd camp overnight in Provo Canyon. We soon left Provo behind, except for an occasional farmhouse, and after half an hour I pointed to a plateau to the east of us. "Moses, don't you think that would be a good place for a college?"

"No place is a good place for a school," he said with disgust.

"Well, I'll bet someday the church will build a big school there, with a wonderful temple up on the hill."

"Nah, they'd never do that," he said with a laugh. "It's too far from town!"

I smiled and kept quiet about the future, as Brigham had requested, but it would've been fun to fill this young boy's mind with ideas and inventions he'd never imagined! Instead, I steered our conversation to the scenery and the chores he did each day.

We soon entered Provo Canyon, and I was thankful a series of bridges had recently been built across the Provo River, so we were able to stay out of the water. I noticed Will always stayed several yards ahead of us and rarely looked back. "Is Will always this serious?" I asked.

"Don't you know why Will is guiding us rather than one of my other brothers?"

"No. I hadn't even thought about it."

"It's because he's already asked for someone's hand in marriage. Papa knew he wouldn't try courting you."

"What do you mean?"

"All my brothers and their friends saw you riding with the prophet as you came into town, and they all said you were pretty. They wanted to meet you at last night's meeting, but you never showed up." He laughed and slapped his thigh. "Those were some disappointed boys! When Papa overheard them talking about you, he knew Will and I were the only ones he could trust to not bother you. Will's girlfriend wasn't happy, but that's life!"

I was glad Moses couldn't see my face because I knew I was blushing. Growing up, I'd been well-liked by everyone and had been in school singing groups, but I wasn't one of the "popular" girls. I rarely even dated. So it was a little overwhelming to realize I had all my peers' great-grandfathers swooning over me—with mud in my hair, no less!

We heard a low rumble farther up the canyon. I asked Moses what it was, but he just said, "You're going to like this!" We rounded one final outcropping, and I gasped as we peered up at a towering torrent of water—Bridal Veil Falls.

I'd seen the falls before, of course, but I'd always been zooming by at 60 miles per hour on the highway. Now we were so close that the mist blew against our faces. Will had tied his horse to a tree and was climbing the hill to the bottom of the falls. We followed him, and within minutes we were standing on the edge of a pool formed over the centuries by the relentless water. We were beneath the shadow of the mountain, and the thick mist soaked our clothes. Will had hiked even farther along the pool, nearly hidden from our view by the rushing water.

"I don't want to go any closer," I said. "It looks too slick."

"We'll be fine," Moses said. We held hands and carefully climbed across the rocks to Will's side. He turned his gaze from the bubbling, churning water and gave us an excited look. "Are you ready, Moses?" he said. "Last time we came you were too little."

"I'm ready! Come on, Emma!" They each took one of my hands and tugged me toward the edge of the waterfall. "What are you doing?" I shouted.

"Going under the waterfall!"

I shrieked in protest, pulling away from them and nearly tumbling down the rocky slope. They quickly grabbed me again and tried to calm me down. "It's really easy," Will said. "Watch!" He left me with Moses, then climbed a ledge near the falls. He stuck his arm into the waterfall, then vanished inside it!

"Come on in," Will yelled from behind the waterfall. My curiosity overpowered my fear, and I allowed Moses to lead the way. When we reached the falls, Moses let me slip past him, and I grabbed onto Will's hand, which he'd extended to me through the curtain of water. I held my breath and stepped forward. I was instantly soaked, and shockingly cold water pummeled my head. Then I was through, with Moses right behind me. We found ourselves against a huge cliff, with water cascading down just inches above our heads. I extended my hand, letting the waterfall shoot through my fingers.

"What a great hideout!" Moses said.

"It's so nice and cool in here," I said as we gazed out at the sunlit canyon through the shimmering waterfall. "I don't want to go back into that heat."

"I'd love to stay all day, but we better get back on the trail," Will said. "There's still plenty of riding ahead of us."

"Let me wash out my hair," I said. I undid my ponytails and ruffled my hair with my fingers, then stuck my head into the waterfall. The cold water numbed my head, but it was refreshing, especially since I knew I wouldn't be getting another shower for quite a while.

Later that evening Will chose a campsite along a small stream in a side canyon—the canyon that would someday lead to Sundance Ski Resort. The boys had brought along a piece of canvas, and after building a teepee out of tree limbs, they wrapped the canvas around the limbs to create a shelter. Will cut some pine boughs, then took blankets from his horse's pack. He placed the blankets over the branches, making a nice little bed.

"You two will sleep in here," he said. "I'll build a place for myself downstream."

Moses started a campfire, lighting it with flint and steel. This eight year old really amazed me, but he seemed accustomed to heavy responsibilities in helping the Saints tame this wilderness. He looked up at me and asked, "How about gathering up some firewood for tonight?"

I found a few branches on the ground, but I quickly realized I had a severe case of saddle sores. My thighs were blistered, and I could hardly walk. "I guess you haven't ridden many horses," Moses laughingly called out.

That was an understatement. My previous riding experience was a three-minute donkey ride at a county fair. I dragged the branches back toward the fire and gingerly sat down on a rock. "I feel like I sat in a hornet's nest!"

"You'll get used to it in a week or so," Moses said. I could only groan.

Once the fire was roaring, Will returned from building his shelter. We heated up the rest of the stew Rachel had made the night before, and it still tasted great! We took drinks from the stream, then settled in for the night. Moses curled up in a blanket and was snoring softly within minutes. I lay awake listening to the crickets, pondering this wild journey. I was only a few miles from where I'd grown up, yet I was separated from anyone I'd ever known. Will and Moses were pleasant company, but it was comforting to know I'd soon be with people I could call family.

Soon after daybreak, I poked my head out of the shelter and saw the boys frying some trout over the fire. "Hello, sleepy-head," Moses said. "Will has already caught breakfast for us."

I sat on a log next to Will, and he handed me a plate holding two fish. "Just tear pieces off with your fingers," he said, "and watch for little bones." I tore off a piece and nibbled at it. It tasted pretty good! I quickly finished off the two fish and then another.

"Hey, leave some for us!" Will said teasingly. "Do I have to go catch some more?"

"I could've eaten another one," I said, "but I'm ready to get back on the trail."

Will reached into his pack, then tossed me a sack filled with deer jerky. "I brought this along for you," he said. "I heard that despite your small frame, you have quite an appetite!"

"Oink, oink!" Moses said. "Is that why you were covered with mud?"

"Are you calling me a pig?" I playfully shoved him off the rock he was sitting on.

Will stepped between us. "That's enough! It's time to get going." Then he gave us a sly smile. "Besides, you both eat like pigs!"

Our playful banter during breakfast put us in a good mood, and my legs even felt better. We quickly packed and hit the road again. By mid-morning we emerged from the rocky canyon into a narrow valley. Deer Creek Reservoir's large dam had always marked the end of Provo Canyon for me, so it was strange to keep following the river, since this area is now submerged.

"By the way, do you know where the Daltons live?" Will asked.

All I knew was their farm had been covered up by the east end of the reservoir. "I think if we stay on the road, we'll come across it," I said. "It's a few miles west of Heber in a settlement called Charleston. I know they live near the river."

Late in the afternoon, we approached a small farmhouse with a fairly new barn. I suggested we stop at the house to see if they knew the Daltons. We tied our horses to the front fence, and I knocked on the door. We heard chairs screech across the floor, and in a moment a slender man with light brown hair opened the door. I felt relief and surprise because this man was the spitting image of my grandpa's brother Lanny!

"Hello, we're looking for the Dalton farm," I said. "This must be it!"

"It sure is," the man said with a British accent. "May I help you?"

I grabbed his hand, barely holding back tears. "I am Emma Dalton, and I have traveled a very long way to find you!"

"You're a relative, then," the man said. "Come right in and make yourselves comfortable. I'm Finity Dalton."

We were warmly welcomed by Finity, his wife, Mary, and their several children. They invited us to eat dinner with them, and Will and Moses kept them entertained with stories from "down in the valley." As we finished the meal, Will said, "Thank you for dinner, Sister Dalton. We hate to leave, but Moses and I really need to start back while there's still some sunlight. Dad wanted us back by tomorrow night."

I protested, but they felt it was best. I walked out to the horses with them and thanked them for guiding me through the canyon. "Maybe we'll see you again," Moses said.

"I hope so, but if not, whenever I see a waterfall, I'll think of you."

They hopped on their horses and waved good-bye, then galloped down the canyon, literally disappearing into the sunset.

Chapter Seven

I returned to the house and found that Finity had gone into the kitchen to help Mary clean up dinner. I grabbed a few cups off the table and took them to the big washtub where they were cleaning the dishes. Mary, a heavy-set, dark-haired woman with brown eyes, gave me a kind smile. "How was your trip, dear?" she asked. "That road can be rough sometimes."

"I'm a little sore, but that's to be expected."

Finity motioned for me to sit on a small wooden barrel, then said, "We're glad to hear more Daltons are arriving in the West. Where's the rest of your family?"

"I came alone. I don't think you'd know my parents. They are Mark and Michelle." They thought for a moment, then shook their heads. "No, we don't know them," Mary said. "Were they from Lincolnshire?"

"Their families were from England, but my parents have been living in the United States for most of their lives." How desperately I yearned to reveal my true identity, but I knew that wouldn't be wise, and I tried to contain my excitement. I was actually talking with my great-great-great-great-grandparents! I'd seen unsmiling black-and-white photos of both Finity and Mary, but these two were nothing like that. Here they were in living color, with Mary scrubbing grime out of a pot and Finity drying off a plate. I knew their first two years in Zion had been very difficult, such as living in a muddy cave during their first winter, but they really didn't look any worse for the wear. They seemed happy with life, and they were very curious about this relative who'd dropped into their lives.

"So how are we related?" Finity asked.

"I'm a descendant of your grandfather Joseph Dalton, but since I've spent my whole life in America, I haven't met any of our relatives."

"That's a surprise," he said. "I didn't know any of Grandpa Joe's kin had come to America."

Mary placed the pot on a shelf, then came to my side. "Then what has brought you to the middle of nowhere?" she asked. "Are you a Latter-day Saint?"

"Most certainly." That brought smiles from both of them. "In fact, I have a letter from President Brigham Young addressed to you in my behalf."

They exchanged startled looks, and Finity jumped up to receive the letter. "I haven't read it yet," I said, "so if you wouldn't mind, please read it to us."

Finity opened the letter and glanced through it first. He cleared his throat and said, "Yes, it looks like something that concerns all of us." He then read the following letter.

Dear Finity,

I send you this letter as a brother in the Lord, and I hope all is well.

I made the acquaintance of Miss Emma Dalton yesterday, and I spoke with her about a very important errand the Lord has required of her. The Lord desires that Emma travel to Denver, in Colorado territory, to obtain some valuable information. I feel impressed that you or another family member must help Emma reach Denver, find the information she needs and then return again. I realize that it is nearly harvest time and every able hand is needed.

But Emma's mission is of much greater importance than that of wheat and corn, or I wouldn't ask such a thing of you. The Lord is pleased with you, Finity, and I know you will honor this call from the Lord.

Your brother in the gospel,

President Brigham Young

The room was silent as he concluded the letter. I think Finity and Mary were pondering how they could fulfill this call from the prophet, but in my mind I kept hearing Brigham's words, "Emma's mission is of much greater importance than that of wheat and corn." Until this moment, the purpose of this strange adventure hadn't really sunk in. But now I felt called and empowered by the Lord, much like a full-time missionary does. I also knew I'd remain in the 1860s until I found the information I sought.

Finity folded the letter and tapped it against his leg. He looked at Mary, who gave him a firm nod. Then he turned to me. "Emma, this puts us in a bit of a bind, but we will do what the Lord's prophet has asked."

"I can take care of the farm while you go," Mary said.

"I know, and you'd do fine, but we've got a big crop this year," Finity said. "I need to stay to oversee the harvest. But this errand in Denver can't be put off until after the harvest because the winter storms in the mountains would be deadly."

Finity paused, pondering the situation. He reopened the letter. "The prophet does say another family member could go..."

"Send George," Mary said. "He could do it."

"But he's just a boy!"

"Don't forget he's 16 now," Mary said. "Besides, he knows the way to Fort Bridger. We need him here, and it would break my heart if something happened to him, but the Lord needs him, too."

I sat silently, listening to them work it out. I hadn't realized what such a trip would require. My father and his brothers once went to a Colorado Rockies baseball game in Denver, and they made the round trip in a little over two days. I knew we wouldn't be zooming along I-70 as Dad did, but I hadn't considered the sacrifice this trek would require of the Daltons.

Mary put her hand on mine. "Emma, this is a bit hard for us because we have had five sons, but only two are still living. We lost two little boys to illnesses, and then our oldest, Robert, died on his way here from England. He had stayed behind when the rest of us came because we couldn't all afford to come. Then when he came on his own, he disappeared while rabbit hunting along the trail."

She paused, letting her emotions settle. "So the only sons we have left are George and 10-year-old William, and the thought of sending another son out on that trail makes me hurt, especially since we rely so much on George. We'd really miss him."

We waited for Finity's response. He sat quietly for a minute, then said, "You're right. George is the one to go. We'll survive the harvest if I hire one of the Giles' boys to help out, but I don't like the idea of two youngsters traveling alone all the way to Denver. That's a rough trip for well-equipped wagon trains, much less two people on horseback. Who else could also go who is a little older and has some outdoor experience?"

"How about that North boy?" Mary said.

"Which one? David? He'd be a good choice," Finity said. "Jesse would never let him go, though, especially since David's left hand is banged up from that wagon accident last week." Finity smiled and shrugged. "Then again, it's not easy to harvest crops with a hurt hand."

"He's the one," Mary said firmly. "David is useless to Jesse, but he'd be invaluable to Emma and George." She turned to me. "I don't know what awaits you on this journey, but the Holy Ghost has filled my heart ever since Finity read that letter. We'll help you all we can."

Tears came to my eyes as I watched these wonderful people work together in my behalf. They had no idea that their descendants for generations to come would revere their names. Right now, like any righteous couple, they were just trying to follow the Lord's prophet. I gave Mary a tight hug. "I've felt so alone, but I feel so close to both of you."

"Don't get so worked up, dear," Mary said, stepping back and taking both of my hands in hers. "I hate to say it, but after what we've been through the past few years for the Lord's kingdom, it was starting to feel a little quiet around here, wasn't it, Finity?"

Finity nodded with that grin on his face that would travel through the gene pool. "I was starting to wonder if the Lord felt he couldn't count on us anymore," he said. "I'm always grateful when the Lord requires something of us, because it means we're still on his good side!"

Chapter Eight

The next two days were a blur as we prepared for a two-month trip. I didn't have any idea where to begin, but all the Daltons rallied together, and soon everything was ready to go. My denim jumper and sandals weren't holding up very well, so Mary gave me two of her dresses and some sturdy shoes, along with two pairs of women's underwear. I knew the dresses had been painstakingly made by hand, and I appreciated Mary's generosity.

Finity had immediately gone down the road after our first conversation to talk with his neighbor Jesse North. At first, Jesse was reluctant to let his son go with us, but Finity let him read the letter from Brigham, and he soon changed his mind.

So our little traveling party consisted of my great-great-great-grandpa George Dalton, 19-year-old David North, and me. We'd each ride a horse, and we'd take along two more supply horses. I was worried about handling a horse by myself, so George spent an afternoon coaching me in the art of horseriding and how to care for the animals. I was given a gentle brown mare named Molly to ride, but after an hour of practice I still had trouble getting Molly to respond to my commands. George finally had me get off the horse and stroke Molly's nose.

"Molly knows you're nervous," George said. "Just talk to her and get to know her."

I felt a little strange, but I did as he directed. As I petted her nose and neck, I said, "Molly, my name is Emma. We're going to be spending a lot of time together, so we need to trust each other." I soothingly spoke to Molly for a few more minutes, then got back in the saddle. Molly now responded to all my movements with the reins, and we were soon trotting around the farm.

"I think Molly likes you!" George called out. "You'll make a good team."

George had a stocky build, and he combed his brown hair

over to the side. His blue eyes shined when he smiled, but for the most part he took life seriously. Mary had told me that George had taken the death of his brother Robert very hard. But rather than mourning very long over the loss, George had quickly become Finity's right-hand man. He'd be a good guide for us.

Now all we were waiting for was David's arrival. His father had decided to make him paint their new barn before he departed, so David hadn't even come to the Daltons' farm yet. George had gone over to talk with him, and he said David was eager to go, especially since it would put a halt to his tedious one-handed painting job.

The Daltons' only daughter still at home, 12-year-old Elizabeth, had helped me pack my belongings, and we became friends. She was a bright, pretty girl, but she was also a tease, so I never knew when to take her seriously. For example, as we waited for David to arrive, she took me aside and gave me a warning.

"I must tell you that David can be repulsive," she said in a low voice. "You might not be able to tolerate him. He smells like a skunk and has the face of a badger." As I gasped, she added, "He shuffles along like a bear, but you'll be riding on horses, so you won't have to worry about him keeping up." She patted my shoulder in sympathy, then entered the house to do her chores.

What kind of creature had Finity saddled us with? Was David the only person he could find to help us? I fussed with the saddle buckles on one of the supply horses and kept grumbling to myself. Maybe David shouldn't go after all! George and I could make it alone.

A tap on my shoulder snapped me out of my mental whining. I turned around and gazed up into the most gorgeous blue eyes I'd ever seen. I also noticed the tanned, clean-shaven face, sandy brown hair and strong shoulders that surrounded those eyes.

"Uh, hello," I stammered. "May I help you?"

"Could you show me which horse is mine?" the man asked.

"What do you mean?" Then I saw his bandaged left hand.

"Are you David North?"

"Yes, and you must be Emma," he said graciously. "I'm happy to see you're more pleasant-looking than the pitiful girl Elizabeth described when she visited me yesterday."

"Why, thank you. It's a pleasure to meet you, too."

We took a moment to size each other up, both glad that Elizabeth's descriptions had been total nonsense. Suddenly feeling self-conscious, I said, "The horse by the barn is yours. Would you please excuse me?" I walked directly into the house, where I could see Elizabeth laughing just inside her bedroom door. She tried to slam the door, but I forced the door open, then shut it behind us. Elizabeth ran to the bed, where I caught her and began tickling her until she could hardly breathe. I was a bit angry, but also amused at the boldness of this prankster.

"That was no badger's face I saw out there, Elizabeth! Why didn't you tell me he was handsome?"

Elizabeth pushed me away, then said, "Weren't you less nervous waiting for a scary troll than you would've been waiting for the real David?"

"I suppose, but why did you tell him I was ugly?"

She squirmed a little. "I just wanted to make sure he's going on this trip for the right reasons, and not because he knows there's a pretty girl going with him. He passed the test."

"Doesn't he have a steady girlfriend?"

"Not yet. There are a few girls interested in him, but the Norths have only been here since May. The family lived in Salt Lake before President Young asked them to come here, and it has taken a lot of time to get their land cleared. So David hasn't had time for socializing." She paused, then slyly added, "Besides, he's waiting for me."

My jaw dropped. Elizabeth had a crush on David! I could understand why, but she seemed way too young to start thinking that way. Maybe her "test" of David wasn't benevolent after all.

"Why are you worried?" I asked. "I don't have any interest in David." She gave me a skeptical look, but I pushed on. "He is just helping us on our trip. Besides, in my time guys rarely gave me a second thought. Why would that change now?"

Elizabeth raised her eyebrows. "What did you say?"

Wow, that was a slip of the tongue. "What I meant to say is when I was younger, boys didn't have much interest in me."

"That's not what I saw from the front door." The playfulness between us had evaporated. "Someone sure is interested in you now," she huffed. "You need to make it plain to him that you aren't interested in him at all." Then she stood up and left the room.

She had a good point—I'd felt an immediate attraction between David and me. I felt queasy, realizing I would be spending two straight months with this man. How many times would I make a klutz out of myself before he lost interest in me?

Hold on! What was I thinking? This wasn't my appointed time on earth! I'd surely return to modern times somehow. My mind told me this journey's purpose was to gather genealogical information, but my heart was telling me otherwise. Oh, this could get messy!

Our journey to Denver began on a peaceful Monday morning in late July 1868. We passed through Heber, then followed a trail along the Provo River for several miles. Since we each rode our own horse, we didn't do much talking during the day. George took the lead, with me in the middle and David following behind. Our two supply horses were tied by a long rope to David's saddle. I would glance back at David occasionally, but he acted as if I weren't even there. I was smitten by him, and it hurt to be ignored.

As we set up camp that night, David finally warmed up to me. "So how did Elizabeth describe me to you?" he asked.

"Quite accurately," I said with a laugh. "She said you smelled like a skunk, had the face of a badger, and you shuffle everywhere you go."

"Really? Yes, that's pretty close."

George coughed on a piece of jerky, then laughingly spit it into the fire. "Elizabeth's quite the storyteller," he said. "Mama thinks the devil's got her tongue."

David nodded. "Sister Dalton might be right about that, because Emma's a bit different than Elizabeth described."

""What do you mean?" I asked.

"She told me you had wrinkled skin, evil eyes, and brayed like a donkey."

"That little weasel!" I squealed.

"I guess she was right about the voice," David said. I pouted a little, and he gave me a little punch in the arm. "We're just teasing you," he said. Well, he wasn't ignoring me anymore, but now he was treating me like a little sister. Which was worse? So much for romance.

George and David shared a large tent, while I slept in a small tent situated between them and the fire. We kept this arrangement throughout the trip, and I enjoyed watching the flames dance across the tent canvas each night as I pondered what might await us in Denver.

As we traveled through the mountains, we encountered all kinds of animals. During the day, we would sometimes find dozens of deer blocking our path. The deer would stare at us as we approached. Then one would bolt away, triggering a chain reaction as they all scampered along the hillside. Many birds seemed intrigued by us, chirping loudly as we worked our way up the mountain trail. During the night, we would hear animals lurking around the tents, such as skunks, foxes and squirrels. We made sure our tent flaps were securely tied shut, and since the men kept our food supply in their tent, these nocturnal visitors rarely found anything to eat.

As we settled down to sleep after our fifth day on the trail, we could hear the horses getting restless and excited. Then we heard angry hissing and growling coming from near the horses! It scared me out of my wits! I heard David and George climb out of their tent. They started shouting and banging rocks together, and they quickly rebuilt the smoldering fire. The fire was soon roaring, and I cautiously left my tent.

"What would make a sound like that?" I asked.

"It sounded like a cougar," David said. "It was probably drawn to us by the horses. I don't think it will return now that we've got the fire going."

The next morning we walked up the hillside to where we'd heard the hissing. Sure enough, there were several cougar paw prints in the soft mud just 20 yards from the horses. During the rest of our time in the mountains, we went to sleep each night with the fire piled high and burning brightly. This also helped reduce our nightly visits from the pesky foxes and skunks. The crackling fire made it a little harder to get to sleep, but it was much more comforting than lying there in the dark waiting for a cougar to pounce on me.

Chapter Nine

We really felt like we were making progress once we reached the Mormon Trail. The trail we'd used from Heber had been rough in places, but the Mormon Trail had been in constant use for more than two decades, and we enjoyed the smoother path. Since we didn't have a wagon to pull, we covered a lot of ground, sometimes traveling 30 miles a day.

I loved to wave to families as they passed us on their way to Salt Lake City. We seemed to be the only group heading east, but there was a continual flow of traffic heading to Zion. There was an occasional fancy wagon carrying a distinguished man and woman, but most travelers rode in simple canvas-covered wagons. The parents would sit up front, with a few younger children hanging out the back. The older children walked behind, sometimes herding a cow. Some of the kids didn't even have shoes, but they would happily chatter with us as they passed by. Their excitement was contagious.

"Why are they so happy?" I asked.

"They're going to be with the Saints," George said. "I remember that wonderful feeling. After traveling so far, they sense they're almost to Zion."

"It's great to see hundreds of Saints still coming each year," David said. "I was born in Salt Lake, but Mom and Dad still talk about their journey across the plains. It's nice to finally see where they traveled."

"When we came in 1864, we took the train all the way to Iowa, but it was still a pretty good trek," George said. "I hear the railroad has reached into Wyoming Territory now, so these people don't have so far to walk. That would've been great!"

"Isn't the railroad supposed to reach Salt Lake next year?" David asked.

George and I said "yes" at the same time, and they both

looked at me. "Well, that's what I've heard," I said.

"How did you get here, Emma?" David asked. "I've never thought to ask."

"Well, I've spent a lot of my life in Springville," I said, a little flustered.

"Did your family come by wagon?" David asked.

"Yes, well, no. I mean, I walked awhile. Then I rode in a wagon. Oh, never mind!"

How could I explain it? I stuck my heels in Molly's ribs and shot out ahead of them. I glanced back, and they were shrugging and laughing. I heard David exclaim, "I'll never understand women!" Then I rode out of earshot for a while.

I spotted three Indians on horseback watching us from a hill, and I decided to rejoin the men. I pointed to the Indians, and David said, "They seem content to just watch us, but keep an eye on them."

George got a smile on his face. "That reminds me of one night on the farm last fall," he said. "We had some Indians sneak down to the corral and try to steal our animals. We scared them off, but in the morning one of our pigs was happily running around with an arrow through its ear!" We all laughed, and it somehow eased my fears a little.

Within a few days we climbed out of the mountains and started across the brown hills and barren stretches of Wyoming. The wind seemed to never stop blowing, and our lips soon dried and cracked. The sun was mercilessly hot, and as we reached the crest of each hill, another small valley and brown hill awaited us. We camped out in the open, since there weren't really any trees to shelter us. We were able to pile up and burn buffalo chips at night for warmth, and once in awhile we'd cross a small stream, where we'd refill our water bags, but the monotony was brutal. The song "Pioneer Children Sang As They Walked" barely begins to express the feelings of endless days on the trail.

Life became worth living again one Saturday evening when

we spotted a weathered wooden sign propped along the trail. It read, "Fort Bridger—5 Miles." Hooray! Civilization at last! We camped for the night, and by 8 a.m. the next morning we dropped down into a green valley. Fort Bridger was below us, surrounded by trees with a river passing through it. It looked like an oasis.

Rather than being a fortress, Fort Bridger was more a collection of whitewashed buildings and stables hooked together by fences. The fort had once been sold to the Saints by Jim Bridger, but then the Saints burned it to the ground in an effort to slow down Johnston's Army during the "Mormon War" of 1859. The tactic had worked, and the fort was abandoned for a time. Then Bridger sold the land to the U.S. government, fully knowing it still belonged to the Mormons. The Saints were in no position to reclaim it, so the Army redeveloped it, and now it was a key defense and supply center.

———

I'd kept my spirits up on the trail by imagining a soothing bath at the fort, since the two men had said we'd rest at Fort Bridger. We planned to get our supplies, then spend the remainder of Sunday letting the horses rest and allowing our bodies to recuperate. The other travelers at the fort, however, weren't anything like the gentle pioneers we'd seen on the trail. This was a whole different class of humanity. Near the stables, men stood around in small groups, hooting and hollering. They all had liquor on their breath and gold on their minds. The gold rush that had started several years earlier in Colorado and Wyoming was still going strong, and Fort Bridger was a lifeline for hundreds of fortune-seekers.

We tied our horses to a hitching post, then stepped inside the small brick supply store. Inside were soldiers, gamblers, and gold-seekers, and the vast majority seemed to be leering at me. The few women I'd seen had wisely stayed outside the store, and I wished I had. I grabbed onto George's left arm and we backed against the far wall. As David purchased the supplies, we listened to the conversations around us.

"They've struck another rich vein of ore on the Sweetwater River," a scraggly man said.

"That's where I'm headed," an equally scary man responded. "I had some luck down on Cherry Creek near Denver, but now I'm moving on to bigger things!"

Nearly every conversation was peppered with profanity, and the main topics seemed to be gold and women. The store was an endless eruption of noise as eager prospectors shouted and bickered in their haste to get what they needed and start back to the mining fields. Despite their hurry, the men found time to smile and leer at me. George held them off by continually repeating, "Get back! Leave her alone! She's with me!"

One tobacco-stained man didn't get the message though, and he reached out to touch my arm. George instantly slugged the man in the chest, knocking him to the ground! The man came up on one knee and spat out a string of vulgarities at us.

"Watch your language around the lady," George said firmly. The man made a weak lunge at George, but George landed a right hook on the man's jaw, and he crumpled to the floor. "Let's get out of here," George said.

We elbowed our way through the crowded store and reached David just as he finished our purchases. We walked to our horses. Then we noticed the man George had hit was talking excitedly to his friends. He pointed at us, and the group started running in our direction.

"David, we need to get out of here fast," George said. "That maggot over there was bothering Emma, so I slugged him. It looks like he's found some reinforcements."

We hopped on our horses and galloped away just as the man and his friends reached the hitching post. They screamed obscenities at us, but we left them in our dust. So much for a restful Sabbath day! My vision of a relaxing bath quickly disappeared. I couldn't have imagined peacefully bathing in that atmosphere. Once we were several miles beyond Fort Bridger, we finally relaxed a little and shared with each other the absurdities we'd seen. By the end of the day, we'd laughed so hard that our sides hurt.

When we left Fort Bridger we had changed trails, leaving the original Mormon Trail and embarking on a new, more direct route across Wyoming called The Overland Trail. Many Saints now used this trail to Zion. It skirted along the bottom of what is now the Wyoming border, eliminating the Mormon Trail's big northerly loop. So while water was less available along this route, it shaved many days off the trip.

Not to say the trip felt shorter. After another 10 days of riding over endless brown hills, we finally reached the town of Laramie. A portion of the railroad had reached the town in the past month, and Laramie was going wild. The town's population had exploded overnight from 300 settlers to 5,000 opportunists. Buildings were being thrown together with whatever people could get their hands on. I saw a small structure built completely out of gun crates!

The main part of the Overland Trail continued east to Cheyenne, but George said he'd heard there was a branch of the trail that headed to Denver from Laramie. We stopped to asked for directions, but it was almost impossible to slow anyone down. We could only watch in amusement as everyone scrambled around us like angry ants. George finally had to grab a man by the shirt. "Hey, can you tell us where the trail to Denver is?"

The man looked annoyed, but he pointed south. "Just head toward those mountains," he said. "You'll find a trail that goes right through them." Then he dashed off. What a strange town!

"What could be so important?" I asked.

"There's money to be made with the railroad's arrival," David said. "The first hotels get the most business. The first saloons sell the most whiskey. You get the idea."

We headed south and found the trail, leaving Laramie's hustle and bustle behind us. George told us the trail had been built by the U.S. Army in 1860, following an ancient Cherokee Indian trail. It was refreshing to see green mountains again after endless days of brown hills.

The first Sunday on the trail, at Fort Bridger, had hardly been restful, and the second Sunday had come when we were in the middle of nowhere. We had rested part of the day, then traveled during the afternoon. So in the past three weeks we had hardly taken a break. As we set up camp the following Saturday evening, George said we ought to take the Sabbath off and let the horses rest. I felt like shouting for joy! I slept better that night than I had in quite awhile.

A glorious sunrise greeted us, and we spent Sunday relaxing and reading out of the Book of Mormon. I was surprised that neither of them had ever read the book. I read to them several of the war-oriented and Three Nephite parts that Doug liked, and the men ate it up.

"That stuff is great!" David said. "After seeing some of the wild folks out here, we might end up using some of those war strategies ourselves."

"Speaking of strategies, Emma, what are we here for?" George asked. "I know President Young asked us to guide you to Denver, but why? Are we looking for more Gold Plates?"

It was a very weak attempt at humor, but he and David started laughing and couldn't stop. I wasn't amused, because I'd pondered that very question for weeks. They saw my stern expression and finally settled down. "It has something to do with my ancestors," I said. They waited for more, so I explained we would be looking for Thomas Cooper and his family.

"Have you ever met any of these people?" George asked.

"No. They're my mother's relatives, and we've tried everything to find them. They have information my family desperately needs, but they seem to have vanished off the earth."

"What makes you think they're in Denver?" David asked.

"I had a dream that gave me direction," I said. "Then President Young gave me his strong assurances." My fortitude weakened as I saw them give each other doubting looks.

"Are you saying we've traveled 400 miles based on a dream?" David said.

"There's more to it than that," I said. "I know we'll find what's waiting for us."

"I sure hope so," David said. "Do these people have land or money? Is that what your family is after?"

"No, they certainly aren't rich." Then I took a moment to ponder David's question. "If we find the information we're looking for, my relatives will be more grateful than we can imagine."

I knew they were confused, but I left it at that. I walked into a nearby grove of trees to pray for guidance. As I prayed, my mind was filled with forgotten facts. I remembered that Thomas Cooper's daughter Esther had married a man named Henry Sheridan. I am a descendant of Esther's brother, Thomas Junior, who disappeared from sight after 1865. So Esther was possibly the only person alive in 1868 who knew the family's history.

My parents had searched the 1860 Census and found Henry and Esther Sheridan living in Rhode Island. But by 1870 they had moved to a small Colorado town called Green Mountain Falls, where they operated a hotel. As I pieced this together, it became clear that the Sheridans were in Denver, and Esther held the answers I sought!

I ran back to camp and told the men about the Sheridans. I was worried about finding anyone in Denver, since I pictured it as a large city, but David and George didn't seem too concerned. "With specific names to ask about, we shouldn't have much trouble finding them," David said.

"But isn't Denver the biggest city in Colorado?"

"I think so, but it isn't too big, probably 4,000 people or so. No settlers even lived in these mountains until the gold rush at Pike's Peak in 1858," David said. "But I'm afraid that every vagabond in the area who isn't panning for gold is probably hanging out in Denver. I've heard they didn't even have a sheriff there for several years."

He threw a stick into the fire and chuckled. "Some of my neighbors in Salt Lake left everything they owned to seek gold out here, and they all returned empty-handed," he said. "They came back instead with some of the wildest tales I've ever heard. Denver could be a bit rough for a lady."

I remembered the kind of men we'd encountered at Fort Bridger, and I felt overwhelmed. David gave me a comforting smile. "Don't worry," he said. "We'll find the Sheridans and get out of town as soon as possible."

As we climbed high into the mountains, dark clouds began gathering in the afternoon. Then at dusk, the heavens opened. Huge raindrops pelted us, leaving large blotches on our clothing. Soon we were drenched in a terrifying downpour. We climbed off our horses and stood against them, hoping for some shelter, but the rain still beat down mercilessly.

"Look at that!" George shouted. We watched a funnel cloud descend in the valley below, touch the ground, and spit trees and dirt into the air before climbing back into the clouds. "We've got to find a place to stay—a farmhouse or something," David said. "This storm could kill us!"

We left the trail and went toward a ridge where we could see lanterns flickering. We fought through the forest, and soon we saw three small shacks ahead of us.

"Stop!" a voice called out. "You don't want to go there!"

"Who said that?" I asked.

A man in a hooded cloak stepped from behind a large rock. The man was tall and stout, bigger than anyone else I'd seen in the 1860s. I noticed his dark whiskers and penetrating blue eyes. "They call this place Virginia Dale," he said. "Those cabins are known as Robber's Roost, and they're filled with evil men who would cause you harm."

The man's sudden appearance had startled us, and now we had no response to his strange statement. He motioned to us. "Follow me," he said. "I know where you can find shelter."

He led us down the trail through some weird rock formations, then guided us to a small cave. A fire was burning just inside the entrance. We tied our horses to a nearby tree, then followed him inside, letting the fire warm us. It was now dark, and the flames created eerie shapes on the cave walls. We stood in silence, waiting for the man to speak. It was his cave, after all. He crouched down in front of the fire, warming his hands. "You can stay here tonight," he said. "They won't find you here."

"Who? We didn't see anyone," I said.

"The robbers—this mountain is full of them. They wait to

attack unsuspecting travelers. The storm seems to have driven them to the cabins. I'm just glad you're safe."

I glanced at George and David, and both seemed dazed, almost reverent. Maybe the storm had left them frazzled. The man stood and shook each of our hands, then said, "It's been a pleasure to meet you. Just make sure you get off the mountain by sunrise."

Before we could respond, he walked out of the cave and into the darkness. I ran to the entrance, but he was gone! I felt goose-bumps cover my body, and I turned to look at the men.

"That was strange," I said softly. Instinctively, we huddled together. David cleared his throat and said, "I've had my doubts about this trip, but not any longer."

George nodded. "Didn't you feel different around him? There was something about him, like when President Young comes to town…"

"That was a servant of the Lord," David said, cutting him off. "I don't understand the purpose of this mission, Emma, but you've got people watching out for you." He went to the horses and grabbed our bedding, then said, "We'll be off this mountain by daylight."

The next day we followed the Poudre River out of the canyon and into a small mining town that consisted of a few rickety wooden shacks. We could see men working along the river, panning for gold. Other men were on the hillside digging a mineshaft and sending the soil through sifters, searching relentlessly for shiny metal.

We stopped at a trough on the town's main road and watered the horses. There was a heavyset man in a dark suit sitting on a nearby porch. He soon wandered over to us and patted one of our horses. He oozed self-importance, and I disliked him immediately. He took a long drag on his cigar, blew the smoke in our faces, then asked, "Did you just come out of that canyon?" We said yes, and he rubbed his chin thoughtfully.

"You didn't see anyone up there?" he asked. "Nobody said hello or nothing?"

We shook our heads, wishing he'd leave. Instead he just chuckled, his big belly heaving up and down. "You're some lucky folks. That's Robber's Roost up there. Those guys are always looking for fresh blood. Only fools would go through that canyon in a group smaller than 20 people." My dislike for this man was growing steadily.

The man glanced at David's injured hand, snorted in disgust, then moved in front of George. He put his hand on George's shoulder and said, "I'm Isaac Webster. I own this mining operation, and I want you to work for me. We've made thousands of dollars, and I feel in my bones another big strike is coming soon. I'll give you half the gold you find, plus a dollar a day."

I knew this could be a good opportunity for George, even if this disgusting Webster would be his boss, but George didn't even hesitate. "No thanks," he said. "I've got pressing business in Denver."

The man laughed. "What could be more important than striking it rich?"

"I wish you luck," George said, "but mining isn't for me." He then helped me onto my horse, and we rode away.

"That was a very good offer," I said. "Maybe you could work here a few days while David and I are in Denver. The money would help your family."

George looked at me in amazement. "Do you really think I'd just drop you two like sacks of flour and go digging for gold?" he asked. "We're not going to get separated. I'd never forgive myself if something happened to you. Besides, I doubt that man would've upheld his part of the bargain."

He was right. I was foolish to even suggest such a thing. Every conversation we'd heard in the past two weeks had centered on gold, and it was reassuring to know that "gold fever" wasn't going to strike our little group very easily.

As the sun set two days later, we crested a small hill and saw Denver in the distance. The last rays of sunlight glinted off the brick buildings, which jutted sharply out of the flat plain. The Rocky Mountains climbed into the sky a few miles to the west, and two small rivers meandered from the southern mountains and joined in the middle of town. We stopped and gazed upon the scene for a few moments. We were about two miles away from town, and from our vantage point, it looked peaceful and inviting. I expected to reach Denver that night. Finity had given us some money to use, and I figured we'd find a hotel to stay in. I clicked my reins, ready to gallop down the trail, but the men didn't move.

"Let's find a campsite," David said. "We'll go into town first thing in the morning."

I started to protest, but George cut in. "He's right, Emma. That town looks peaceful from here, but within an hour the streets and saloons will be filled with men of all descriptions. I'm a little nervous to wander those streets during the day, much less at night when we don't have any idea where we're going."

I had no choice but to agree. We found a grove of trees and settled in for the night. I didn't sleep much, knowing the information I sought was so close. But if I'd known what awaited us, I may have never left that grove.

Chapter Ten

By sunrise we'd eaten breakfast and packed our tents. We could all sense something important awaited us. As we were about to get on the horses, David stopped us. "I hope today will go smoothly, but I feel we should offer a special prayer," he said. "This could be like looking for a needle in a haystack."

We all knelt as David offered a heartfelt prayer, asking for protection and guidance. As he prayed, I realized that these two expected Denver to be equal to Sodom and Gomorrah. During the slow days on the trail, David and George had jokingly told stories they'd heard of Denver's drunken brawls and riotous living. Although Denver was becoming more civilized, it was still the West's capital of corruption. In our day, Denver has a beautiful temple and a thriving LDS Church membership, but in this day we were likely the only Mormons within 100 miles. We'd enjoyed those wild stories about Denver, but none of us were laughing now.

We quickly reached the outskirts of town, and I noticed saloons easily outnumbered other businesses. The town was barely stirring at that early hour, and we had the wide, dusty streets to ourselves. Not even the tumbleweeds were moving.

"Where is everyone?" I asked.

"I suppose they're still sleeping off a night of 'wine, women and song,'" David said. "That might help us, though. The shopkeepers will be awake, and they'll be more helpful than someone who's shaking off a rough night. Let's start talking to people on this next block. Emma, you could hold the reins of the horses while George and I work our way down each side of the street."

I slowly led the horses along as George and David stepped into each building, asking people if they knew a Sheridan family. By noon, they'd asked at more than 80 places with no luck. The streets were getting crowded, and I was having a hard time keeping our horses out of the way. I was discouraged, and I called the men over to me. "Let's take a break," I said. "I need to sit down. Plus I'm starving."

We tied the horses to a hitching post outside a nearby saloon and walked inside. This certainly wasn't McDonald's. The room was dimly lit, and the stench of cigar smoke crowded out any other smells. We took a table in the corner, and David went to the bar to order us a meal before joining us. George and David had stayed optimistic all morning, but their initial excitement had long worn away.

"Did you find any real clues?" I asked.

"One storekeeper said a Sheridan woman comes there once a week, but he didn't know her first name and had no idea where she lives," David said.

"I had about the same luck," George said. "One bartender said a man named Sheridan used to go there a few nights a week, but he hasn't seen him in nearly a month."

"Well, that gives us hope there's a Sheridan family here," I said.

"If they're still here," George said quietly.

A rough-looking woman with horribly bright makeup and a very short skirt came to the table carrying three plates filled with juicy steaks and mashed potatoes. She set them down and asked, "What'll it be? Beer, wine or whiskey?"

"We'll just have water," I said. She shrugged, then brought us three glasses and a pitcher of dark brown water.

"Look at that stuff!" I said. "Did she get that out of a puddle?"

"Maybe we should've taken the beer," George said, only half-jokingly.

David was unfazed, though, and he poured himself a glass and drank it down. He smacked his lips. "Hmm. A little warm, but not bad!" he said. "Give it a try."

He poured himself another glass of the swirling liquid, then filled our glasses. I'm certain something grotesque was swimming in that water, but I was parched, so I stuffed my mouth with potatoes and took a big drink. That method worked quite well, and it kept the others entertained.

I began to put another big scoop in my mouth when a short, chubby man walked up to our table. He had a greasy brown beard and a wide-brimmed hat jammed on so tightly we could barely see his eyes. He looked casually around the saloon, then put one of his grimy hands onto the table. He looked at me and said quietly, "The word around town is you're looking for Henry Sheridan."

"Yes, we need to talk with him," I said. "Do you know him?"

He grinned, showing us a row of tobacco-stained teeth. "Finish your meal, then meet me outside. I'll take you to him." He rapped his knuckles twice on the table as if he'd sealed a deal, then he walked through the saloon's swinging doors.

I was so elated that I danced in my seat. "See? I knew things would work out!"

"I'd like to think we're done knocking on saloon doors, but that guy smelled like trouble," David said. "I don't trust him. We can find the Sheridans ourselves."

George also looked doubtful about the man, but he said, "I'll do what Emma wants."

"What's your worry?" I said. "Here's the answer to our prayers!"

"Well, I guess it can't hurt to hear what he has to say," David said.

We paid for our meal and walked back out into the bright sunlight. We saw our new friend about a block down the street, signaling to us. We decided to leave our horses tied up in front of the saloon, and as we neared the man, he stepped through a door into a warehouse. He beckoned us inside a small storage room. "Come get out of the sun," he said. "Henry will be here soon."

I stepped in ahead of the others, and I heard the door shut behind us. Almost instantly I heard a sickening "Whack!" followed by a bone-crunching "Crack!" I turned to see both David and George slump to the ground! A hulking man stood over them, cautiously poking at them with a thick wooden club.

"They won't be going anywhere, Larry," the man said.

Our short, chubby "friend," who I figured was Larry, looked delighted. "Good job, John. Now tie them real good." David started to stir, and John walloped him once more in the head, knocking him out cold. Then John began wrapping a long rope around them both, tying them to each other.

I'd been too horrified by the sudden violence to even move, but now I bolted for the door. Larry jumped in front of me, grabbed my shoulders and threw me down on top of a crate. I kicked him and screamed, but he smacked me hard across the mouth. "Shut up!" he shouted. "I'd hate to use that club on you."

I quit fighting, and he soon had me tied to the crate in a sitting position. I tried to stay quiet, but I couldn't help whimpering. Larry looked at me angrily. "I told you to keep your mouth shut!" He picked up a filthy rag off the floor, forced open my teeth and wedged the rag deep into my mouth. I was sure I'd vomit any second. Feelings of despair crushed down on me. Why had I brushed aside David's worries? If these were the kind of men associated with Henry Sheridan, maybe this journey was a huge mistake.

———

After John finished tying up the others, he left the warehouse to locate Henry. Larry leaned against the door with a satisfied grin. "I'm glad we found you before you stirred up trouble. Henry didn't intend to kill anybody, but that guy tried to steal our share of the gold from the Poudre River claim."

I looked at Larry incredulously. Henry Sheridan had killed somebody? There had to be two Henry Sheridans in Denver, because I couldn't imagine anyone related to me being a killer. Oh, who was I kidding? All I knew about Henry was what Mom had found in the census, and the census didn't have a category for "evil."

"You better hope Henry has calmed down since I last saw him," Larry said. "Unless you promise to leave him alone, that rope will become a noose around your skinny neck."

A chill passed through me, and I tried desperately to work

the rag out of my mouth, but it wouldn't budge. I jerked back and forth against the rope, but it only caused rope burns across my arms. I felt helpless, and my only friends in this lawless town were unconscious.

"Just settle down!" Larry said wearily. "You'll get plenty of chances to talk when Henry gets here."

Chapter Eleven

I angrily stared at Larry, but he paid no attention to me as he calmly rolled several homemade cigarettes. I was desperate to talk to him, because his description of Henry as a killer had really upset me. I'd never considered dying during my time in the 1860s. That would ruin everything! And what if my great-great-great-grandpa George died? Would I ever be born? What a mess I'd made.

John soon returned with a fairly handsome man, who had to be Henry, with brown eyes and dark hair. He didn't look as wicked as I'd expected. Larry jumped to his feet and said, "These are the people who've been asking about you, boss. They seem to be alone."

Henry came up to me and pulled the rag out of my mouth. "Just keep quiet, and we won't hurt you," he said. I sat quietly, and he watched me for a moment. "I expected a group of Webster's meanest friends to come chasing after me, not three unarmed youngsters," he said with a sad smile. "All I wanted was my portion of the gold so I could buy a hotel and settle down, but that bloated serpent tried to sneak away. What did he plan to do with it all? There's plenty for everyone."

I shrugged and said, "I don't know what you're talking about. We met an Isaac Webster along the Poudre River, but he was a disgusting man, along the lines of Larry."

That unwise remark made Larry angry, and he smashed his fist into my jaw. I saw stars for a few moments, and when I cleared my head, Henry had pushed Larry into a corner and was loudly cursing at him. John watched amusedly from the other corner. For being business partners, these three sure had some communication problems.

Henry noticed I was awake again and came to my side. "I apologize for that idiot's behavior," he said. He glared at Larry sitting in the corner. "That's the same Webster. I just want to work out something to keep us all out of trouble."

"That's all I want," I said. "We only met Webster once for about five minutes. He offered George a job, but that's it. We came to Denver to find out some information about your wife's parents, not recover stolen gold."

He thrust his face in front of mine. "Don't lie to me," he said angrily. "I'm supposed to believe you just happened to meet Webster? You know too much. Who are you, one of his daughters?"

He paced the floor like a caged tiger. "And what do Esther's parents have to do with this? They've been dead for years. Besides, I've caused her enough grief dragging her from Rhode Island. She doesn't need to think about her family, or she might leave!"

He stopped dead in his tracks and pointed his finger at me. "That gold is the only reason why strangers would look for me," he said. "I didn't mean for Webster to die. I heard him packing his bags during the night, and when I tried to stop him, he pulled a knife. I tried to wrestle it away, and we tumbled to the ground. Then blood started gushing out of his chest. He accidentally stabbed himself to death!"

A small sob escaped his throat. Henry looked suddenly very weary, as if he hadn't slept in days. He sat down on a crate across from me. I was too caught up in his story to even whimper. He let out a heavy sigh. "When Webster let out his final scream, one of your men shined a lantern on us and called out my name. I knew I'd be pegged for murder, so I loaded up all the gold my horse could carry and told Larry I'd meet him here. I rode through the night. You're sitting on the crate where some of the gold is hidden."

No wonder I couldn't budge the crate! Larry looked at the crate longingly, probably wishing he'd known the gold's location earlier. I wouldn't trust Larry for a second. I wondered why Henry had hired such a scoundrel.

"I left some gold, and I'm sure your group has divided it," Henry said. "You've probably also divided up my tents and supplies, so I consider us even. I can't believe those fools sent a young girl into town to find me!"

"I have had nothing to do with this Webster guy," I said in despair. "All I want to do is talk to your wife about her family. She knows information about England that I need."

"Are you crazy?" Henry said. "You're not getting near Esther. She's always thought this mining business was foolish, but now I've got some gold. We can make a fresh start."

He obviously wasn't going to let me talk to his wife, so I kept quiet. Henry turned to Larry and John. "I can't risk these three causing me any trouble," he said. "I need them out of the way while I get Esther out of town tonight. The gold in the crate is yours. If you keep these three tied up in the mountains for a few days, I'll track you down next week to give you the rest of your gold."

Larry nodded, but he looked worried. "I don't think we can get them out of town without attracting attention."

Henry pondered that for a moment, then said, "Keep them here until dark, then haul them off." He turned again to me. "I'm sorry we had to meet under such circumstances," he said. "You seem like a nice young lady, but you're not getting the gold, and I'm not facing a murder charge!"

Henry stalked to the door, then slammed it behind him. Once Henry was gone, Larry told John, "I don't care what he says. I'm not going to waste a week watching Webster's kin. We can save a lot of time by pushing them off the cliff in the canyon."

"Why do we have to kill them?" John asked.

"They're holding us back, and I doubt Henry will ever give us the rest of our gold," Larry said. "I'll be content with what's in that crate. After we get rid of these three, I'm heading straight to St. Louis, where I'll buy some land and live high on the hog for the rest of my life."

"I don't feel good about this, Larry."

"I don't care how you feel! Watch them while I get some

supplies. We'll use their horses. I'll be back before dark, and maybe we'll risk an early start."

I kept quiet, not wanting to provoke Larry again. I was too busy praying that we'd somehow survive. I was relieved to realize that Larry, not Henry, was the one with a murderous heart, but that gave me little comfort as I awaited my death at the bottom of a cliff. Larry finally left, and John sat against the door and whittled on a small piece of wood with a pocketknife. It dawned on me that getting John on our side was the only way to save us. It was time to crank up a little feminine charm.

John was carving a small figure, about two inches tall and three inches long. I cleared my throat and said, "Is that a horse you're carving, John?"

He looked up with a surprised smile. "Yeah! How's it looking?"

"Very nice. You're quite talented."

"Thanks," he said. "I'm just finishing it up. I'd give it to you if you weren't going to die tonight."

"You're right," I said. "There's no use giving it to someone who'll never be able to put it on her bedroom dresser." He looked a bit disturbed, and I hoped I'd pricked his conscience. "Anyway, how's the life of a miner?" I asked. "Do you like searching for gold?"

"I liked it when I started working for Henry, but now I hate it," he said. "Everyone gets greedy, and people get killed. All I want now is peace and quiet."

We talked like this for several minutes. He said he felt bad about hitting my friends, and he walked over to the men to check on their wounds. I now felt John could be trusted, so I casually asked him why he obeyed all of Larry's orders. He just shrugged and said, "I'm just a hired hand."

"Do you really want to see us die?"

"No way," he said. "You're a really pretty girl, and I don't believe you'd hang out with Webster." He blushed a little, and I knew it was time to set the hook.

"I've got a plan you might like," I said. "I think you deserve this gold more than Larry, so if you let us escape, you can take this gold and be out of town within an hour. My friends and I will hide out, and you won't get in trouble. Besides, do you really think Larry will share this gold? I'll bet he's planning to send you over the cliff, too!"

John wasn't very bright, but he was smart enough to see I was right. My plan was the only way to save our lives. Plus, it would make him a very rich man. "It's a deal," he said. "Larry's always been cruel to me, and this should settle the score. Let's undo those ropes!"

He untied my rope, and as I worked myself loose, he began unraveling David and George. George snapped awake, and he soon kicked himself free. We had a tough time rousing David, though. Once we got him sitting up, he was disoriented and complained of a severe headache, but it appeared his injuries weren't too severe.

John cracked open the crate and pulled out two canvas bags. He opened one and pulled out a gold nugget the size of a big gumball. "Pure gold," he said, holding it up for us to see. "These bags should set me up for life."

His eyes got a little misty. "I left home when I was 15, and I think it's time to visit my parents in Kentucky. They've had a hard life, and I think a little gold would make them smile."

"That would be very nice, John," I said. "I'm sure your parents would be as eager to see you as they would the gold. I'll bet they accept both."

He smiled and nodded. "I've missed them more than I ever thought I would," he said. I knew exactly how he felt.

John looked at the nugget. Then he flipped it into the air toward George, who caught it. "That's for the damage I did to your head," John said. "Be sure to share it with your friend."

He grabbed the bags and went to the door, then looked back at us. "This is a good plan. I wish I'd thought of it myself. Take care of yourselves."

"Hold on," I said. "Didn't you promise me something?"

John looked confused for a moment. Then he smiled and

reached into his shirt pocket. He pulled out the finely carved horse and handed it to me. "It's yours. I'm glad none of us will die tonight." He poked his head outside, looked both ways, then was gone, hopefully to begin a better life.

Chapter Twelve

Within a minute after John's departure, I cracked open the door. The street was filled with people, but no one seemed to be watching the warehouse. There was an alley at the south end of the building, and my first instinct was to have us scramble around that corner. Then a gentle warning filled my mind, and my eyes focused on a two-story hotel across the street. I ducked back into the room and told the men that I felt we should go to the hotel, reasoning it was the last place Larry would look. They thought I was crazy, but they were in no condition to argue. I checked the street again. Then George and I half-carried David across the road into the hotel lobby.

David and George settled into a couch facing away from the street, and I greeted the desk clerk with a kind, calm smile. "Hello, we'd like a room for the night," I said. He began to register us, and as George stood to pay for the room, I looked back toward the warehouse. Larry was walking up the alley, carrying some supplies! He entered the warehouse, then shot back out the door, hastily looking in both directions. He kicked the dirt like an angry child, then sprinted toward the saloon where our horses were still tied up.

I snatched our key out of the clerk's hand, and we hurried up the stairs to our room and bolted the door. Thank goodness we'd avoided the alley. We would've been tumbling over that cliff by nightfall.

The room's window gave us a good view of the street, and we watched through the curtains as Larry returned to the warehouse. He literally ripped the door off its hinges in frustration, then sprinted back down the alley. Fifteen minutes later he returned and retrieved his supplies. Then he went down the street, hopped on David's horse and led away our horses! I was really upset about losing Molly, and George anguished about how he'd explain this to Finity, but we hoped Larry had given up on finding us. I was sure he'd still return in a few days and try to collect his gold from Henry.

Despite our setbacks, we could still achieve our goal in Denver if we found Esther without running into Henry. But where could she be? Henry had said they'd be leaving that night. Time was running short. I'd nearly asked John where the Sheridans lived, but he might've rejected our deal if he knew we'd still be sneaking around.

So we hadn't made any progress. We'd gained a gold nugget, but we'd lost our horses and become enemies to two unpleasant men. Also, David wasn't doing well. The two hits he'd taken from John's club had done some damage. He'd barely made it up the stairs and was now sleeping on the lone bed in the room. Thankfully, George had recovered. He told me he was going to find where the Sheridans lived, reasoning it had to be nearby.

"George, what if Henry sees you?"

"I doubt he'd recognize me. Besides, he thinks I'm still tied up and under the watchful care of his faithful employees," he said with a grin.

"All right, but please be careful."

George left the room, and I bolted the door behind him. I watched through the window as he crossed the street, gave me a little wave and then entered the corner store. I moved from the window and sat on the bed next to David. I gently touched the two big welts on his head. They were swollen and bruised. He was sleeping soundly, though, so I took the chance to share my feelings with him.

"David, I'm sorry you got hurt. You have helped us so much." I took his injured hand and softly caressed it. "I'm growing very fond of you. You're courageous and wonderful."

I bent over him and kissed his cheek. He stirred slightly, and I flew off that bed like it was electrified! When his eyes opened a moment later, I was sitting serenely in a chair, peering out the window.

"Did you say something?" he asked.

"No, why do you ask?"

"I must've been dreaming." He closed his eyes again and rolled over, completely missing the flustered look on my face.

I scanned the street below for George, but I also watched thick lightning-filled clouds roll toward us across the western sky, threatening to turn the dusty streets into rivers of mud. As dusk approached, George reappeared on the street below. I unlocked the door, and he stepped into the room with a wide smile!

I grabbed him by the arms. "Did you talk with her?"

"No, but I heard her voice," he said. "A lady in the store knew her and gave me directions to their room above McIntyre's Saloon, which is three blocks away. I got bold and decided to go talk with her, but as I got to the door, I heard a man yelling about leaving town immediately. A woman kept saying that Rhode Island's the only place she was going. He called her Esther a few times, so when I was sure it was them, I rushed back here."

"Great job, George!" I exclaimed, giving him a hug. "Now if I can just talk to her alone."

I glanced out the window, and to my surprise Henry was walking down the street! It was barely light enough to see, but when he stopped at the warehouse we knew it was him. He stepped inside for a moment, then came back out looking satisfied. He kicked at the damaged door lying in the street, probably imagining we'd put up quite a fight! Then he walked down the street and entered a horse stable.

My time had arrived. "If I don't go talk to Esther right now, I might not get another chance," I said. "They'll be gone by morning."

"Emma, that's a bad idea," George said. "If Henry sees you talking to his wife, he'll probably kill you! I'll go. That's the safest way."

"No, I need to speak to her in person," I said. "I've already escaped death once today—I can do it again. Let's make a plan."

George shook his head in exasperation, but he agreed to wake up David and get some horses and supplies. George took the gold nugget out of his pocket and studied it. "I sure didn't hold onto this very long, but it'll help us get back on the trail in good shape."

We had no intention of staying overnight in Denver, even though we'd paid for the hotel room. If I obtained the information we sought, we'd leave town immediately. George said they'd wait for me in a vacant lot he'd noticed across from McIntyre's Saloon. He made one more failed attempt to change my mind, then I hurried down the stairs.

I weaved my way through several scraggly looking men and their scantily dressed female friends who were mingling along the wooden sidewalk. I couldn't help but shudder. David was right—this really wasn't a place for a lady! I nearly returned to the hotel, but I pushed aside my fear and jogged out into the street, ignoring the catcalls. I kept reminding myself that talking to Esther was the whole reason I was in this crazy time warp.

I heard McIntyre's Saloon long before I reached it. There was already shouting and clanking bottles coming from inside, and it was barely dark! No wonder Esther was fed up with the Wild West. There was a lantern burning in the second-story window, so I climbed the outside stairway and listened at the door. I couldn't hear anything over the piano playing in the saloon below, but I figured Henry couldn't be back yet. I knocked gently, and within seconds the door swung open to reveal a woman in her late twenties. She bore a slight resemblance to my Grandpa Cooper, and I suddenly felt euphoric. I stepped forward and touched her elbow. "You must be Esther Sheridan."

She recoiled and backed away. "Who are you?"

"I'm a distant relative," I said. "You have some family information that I've been searching for."

She gave me a bothered look, and I noticed her red-rimmed eyes. "Please just go away," she said. "I'm packing things up. My husband and I are going our separate ways."

A tear came to her eye, and she began to shut the door. I quickly threw myself through the doorway, bumping into her. She exclaimed, "Hey! I think you'd better leave!"

I dropped to my knees and said, "Esther, this is extremely important. I know your maiden name is Cooper, you grew up in Rhode Island and your parents are from England. Right?"

That took her by surprise. "Yes," she said cautiously. "How did you know that?"

"As I said, we're distant relatives. My name is Emma Dalton. Can we talk for just five minutes? Anything you can remember about your parents is very important to my family."

She hesitated, then led the way to some rickety chairs near a window overlooking the street. "Ask your questions," she said warily. " I need a break from packing anyway."

I plunged right in. "I'm also related to the Coopers, and we'd like to contact our relatives in England, but no one in my family knows which city your parents came from. Do you remember the specific town they lived in?"

"Of course," Esther said. "They lived in Bristol after they were first married. That's where I was born, and my father's parents, Michael and Sherston Cooper, lived nearby. But my mother's parents, Matthew and Carrie Shumway, lived in Manchester. We only visited them once or twice before we sailed to America. I was seven when we arrived here."

"You're the oldest child in your family?"

"Yes. I have four younger siblings, two still living. Have you met any of them?"

"I thought I'd try to find you first."

"That was wise," she said, warming up to me a little. "I doubt the others even remember those places."

"Speaking of siblings, what ever happened to your brother Thomas Junior? He seems to have disappeared."

She shook her head sadly. "I tried to help that boy, but he wouldn't listen to anyone. When I left Rhode Island last year, he'd just begun serving a 10-year prison term for entering a house, beating up the owner and stealing $2,000 in jewelry. It was the latest of his many problems. His wife and son left him just before the robbery."

"That's terrible! I feel bad for him."

"I don't," she said. "He made his own choices, and now he's paying the price. Don't worry. The rest of the family isn't so criminally minded."

I was fascinated. Esther's mind was loaded with priceless stories, and she didn't even know it. "This is just what our family is looking for," I said. "Has anyone ever written any of this information down?"

She let out a surprised laugh. "Why would we do that? We aren't too proud of Thomas' actions, and Mom and Pop didn't have the best memories of England. We were very poor there, and at times our lives were almost unbearable. That's why we came to America."

Esther had given me everything I needed to know to locate the family in English records, but I wanted to hear so much more. I asked, "What did your father look like?"

I never received an answer. Esther held up her hand for silence, and we heard steps on the stairway. Esther looked alarmed. "Henry was very angry when he left," she said. "You might want to hide somewhere!"

I scrambled to the window, pushed it up, and jumped down to a wooden overhang above the saloon's doorway. The boards squeaked as I landed, but they held. The overhang was about 10 feet long and four feet wide, so I stretched out flat across the rough wood. Esther had the presence of mind to shut the window behind me, and I soon heard Henry's voice. I couldn't hear what he was saying, but he sounded fairly calm. Maybe they'd be able to work things out.

I quit worrying about Esther as I contemplated my own dilemma. The overhang was about 12 feet off the ground, and I didn't want to risk jumping off and breaking an ankle. I didn't really want to move at all, remembering how the overhang had squeaked when I'd jumped onto it. This thing wasn't very stable. Then to make matters worse, those thick clouds I'd watched roll in earlier began to open up. Within minutes I was soaked to the bone. The rain swooped down in torrents, and water ran down the overhang against me. I soon became a human dam, preventing more than an inch of water from running off the overhang onto the street.

I raised up onto my elbows and knees to let the water run beneath me, but one corner of the overhang screeched horribly as I did so. I looked in shock to see only two nails had been used in each corner to hold the awning in place, and the corner near my feet was slowly working loose. Where was the building inspector when this place was thrown together? I had few options, and I knew knocking on the window and facing Henry wasn't one of them.

I decided to work my way to the edge, then hang off and drop to the ground. I shuffled on my stomach over to the edge, but when I put one leg over the side, the entire overhang ripped away from the building! I flattened out on the overhang, and for a moment I felt as if I were riding a magic carpet. Then the overhang began its rapid descent, crashing loudly against the saloon's wooden walkway.

"Owwwww! That hurt," I moaned, and I made no effort to move. My whole body felt broken. The crash brought people out of the surrounding buildings, and, unfortunately, it brought Henry to the window. He took one look at me, then rushed down the stairs. He grabbed me by the back of the dress and pulled me to my feet.

"How in the world are you still around?" Henry screamed. He put an arm around my throat and he seemed ready to finish me off right there. *Bam!* Someone barreled into him, and his grip on me was broken. I saw Esther standing over Henry, who was lying in the muddy street.

"What do you think you're doing, Henry?" she shouted. "This girl came to visit with me, and she has no business with you. Why were you strangling her?"

I put my hand on Esther's shoulder and tried to explain. "Henry thinks I'm here to cause him trouble, but I'm not! We crossed paths earlier today, and he's just surprised to see me again."

"You two have already talked?" Henry asked. We nodded. He got slowly to his feet, with his head hung low. "Esther, I meant for you to hear it from me, but I've got enough gold to give us a comfortable life. Please don't leave me. We can make a good, quiet life together. We'll head south and open up a hotel."

Esther stared at him. "What are you saying, Henry?" she

asked. "Emma didn't mention you have gold."

Henry's jaw dropped as I gave him a cold stare. "We only talked about her parents' life in England, just as I told you," I said. "Now you'll have to tell her the rest."

I could see George and David approaching on horses. Henry glared at them, but he realized it would be best to keep his mouth shut. I turned to Esther and took her by the hand. "Thank you again," I said. "No one else on earth could've given me the information you did."

Esther looked worried. "You remember it all, don't you? Even after your fall?"

"I won't forget it. The Coopers are in Bristol, and the Shumways in Manchester."

"That's right." She gave me a small hug. I whispered in her ear, "I know Henry is a good man at heart. Give him a chance. I think he'll keep his promises."

She looked at me thoughtfully. "As you and I talked, I realized Henry is all I have left," she said. "There's nothing for me in Rhode Island now. We'll give the hotel business a try. You'll have to come stay with us sometime."

She walked over to Henry and put her arm around his waist. "This man is foolish at times, and we fight too much, but I really do love him." Henry stood there silently, with a look of stunned joy on his face. I went over to Henry. "Keep all that gold for yourself," I said. "John took off with the gold in the crate, and Larry left town with our first set of horses."

Henry nodded gratefully. "That's good to know," he said. "We'll head south in the morning."

Esther laughed. "I won't argue with that! I'm tired of saloon music."

I said good-bye, then walked over to the horses, where George helped me into the saddle. The rain was coming down hard, but as we trotted off, I looked back. The crowd had scattered to get out of the rain, but Henry and Esther still stood embracing in the muddy street, ready to give their marriage another try.

Chapter Thirteen

We sloshed our way out of Denver, then finally turned off the trail for the night. David fawned over me, making sure I was all right, and I was relieved to see he was recovering from the beating. As for our "gold fortune," George had a tough time getting a fair price for the nugget in gold-saturated Denver, but finally he had been able to trade the gold for three horses, two tents, some supplies and a little cash. The rain tapered off, and we chatted about our exciting day as we cooked a quick dinner. I hadn't eaten since our lunch in the saloon, which seemed like days ago. I certainly wasn't gaining weight during this trip.

I stood by the fire to let my dress dry out. My other dress had been packed on the horses Larry had stolen, so I'd be wearing this dress the whole way home. The dress smelled smoky, but I didn't mind. I'd smelled like a campfire for weeks now.

We made good time on the trail the next few days. Rain was our companion seemingly every afternoon, but the trail stayed in fairly good condition. We were worried about passing Robber's Roost, but we waited for a strong afternoon rainstorm, then slipped through without a problem. There was a steady stream of people heading south, but we didn't find anyone going our direction until we turned west at Laramie. Some Saints now took the train that far and bought their supplies there. So from that night on we were able to join a Mormon group for dinner before setting up camp nearby. After our experiences in Denver, it was nice to be among Saints again.

We traveled much more quickly on horseback than the Saints did in their wagons, so we spent each night with a different group of church members. It worked out well for us because we had little food, and the Saints were kind to us. George and David would help the men gather firewood and buffalo chips each night to pay for our food, and I'd ask a worn-out mother if I could hold her fussing child. They never refused, and I enjoyed talking with these little children.

One afternoon we came upon a wagon train already circled and preparing camp. With several hours of daylight left, this was unusual, but then we saw the mound of fresh soil near the wagons. The journey to Zion had claimed another victim.

We found the group's leader and asked how we could help. He pointed to a wagon at the far edge of the circle. "That's Brother Chesnut's family. Their father died today. He'd been sick for a week, and he finally took his last breath around noon."

We saw a woman standing at the back of the wagon, trying to prepare food for her children. "His wife Ann is left with four children under the age of seven," the man said. "We told her to rest, but she hasn't sat down since the burial, and she won't take any help. Maybe she'll take some help from strangers."

We walked to the wagon, and David said, "Ann, we've heard about your loss. We're here to help you." She turned to look at us, her face firm and her eyes glazed. Then her face crumpled, and the tears she'd been holding back flowed freely. David took her in his arms as she sobbed. George went to the wagon and finished fixing the meal, and I searched for the children. Three children were sitting quietly in the wagon, mourning their father's death. But where was the fourth child?

I heard a shuffling under the wagon, and I saw a small toddler. He was sitting in the dirt, piling pebbles along the rear wheel. He was covered in dust, and his tear-streaked face was solemn. He wasn't more than two years old, but I saw a great sorrow in his big brown eyes. I crouched down and added a rock to his pile. "Hello there, can I play with you?"

He shook his head a few times and frowned. "No dada," he said. "Dada gone."

My heart cracked as I pulled the little boy from under the wagon and clutched him to me. I carried him outside the wagon circle and found a small rock to sit on. "Yes, your daddy is gone, but he's gone to live with Jesus," I said softly. "He's in a good place."

He looked up at me. "With Jesus?" Hope began to return to his face. "Yes, with Jesus," I said. "Everything will be all right." Those beautiful eyes searched my face. Then he relaxed and cuddled against me. I gently rocked him, and soon he was asleep. David later brought me a plate of food, but I waved him off, not wanting to be disturbed.

I kissed the boy's dirty little cheek and he smiled in his sleep. What a tender boy, enduring such a terrible trial! As I held him, I felt the petty complaints and grudges I'd clung to during my life drain away. I had been so blessed throughout my life—I had no reason to murmur. I held that young boy well into the night before placing him with his siblings in the wagon. His life was forever changed, and so was mine.

The Mormon camps were always full of activity, and I enjoyed the nightly sing-along around the campfire. We discovered the larger groups usually held a makeshift dance each evening, and if it didn't appear the group would hold a dance, we'd suggest it. I learned the Virginia Reel and several other dances, and we had a great time. The first few nights David danced with the 10-year-old girls or the older women, but one night he hooked my arm and pulled me into a spirited square dance. We began dancing together a few times each night, and I got my hopes up again that something might develop between us.

After one really hot day on the trail, I was feeling a bit strange, as if I'd been drugged or suffered sunstroke. I didn't want to miss the dance, though. We heard the fiddle start playing, and I headed toward the music, but George stopped me. "Something's wrong with you," he said. "Why don't you go rest in your tent? We'll be there soon."

"I'm fine," I said defensively, although I was sweating heavily. He backed off, and we joined the Saints. I soon felt a strange urge to liven things up. I told George, "Let's see how the group likes this!"

I did my best moonwalk to the center of the dance area. Then I started doing some moves straight from a bad 1970s episode of American Bandstand. The fiddler stopped in mid-chord, and the Saints looked at me as if I were possessed. I then switched to some modern dance routines my friends had taught me, and now even George and David were giving me looks of disgust. I finished with a cheerleading kick before stumbling to my tent. That was all the modern dancing I did on the trail, and thankfully the incident wasn't mentioned in the morning.

I'd fought against it for weeks, and I knew it wasn't right, but I began to fall deeply in love with David. My previous life seemed so distant, and I had no idea how I was going to return, so I just enjoyed the moment. I could sense that David now looked at me as more than just a friend, but unless we were dancing, he still treated me like a kid sister.

Meanwhile, George was having a pretty good time himself. He was becoming a handsome young man, and I noticed he enjoyed catching the eye of the prettiest available girl, flirting with her a little, then spending the night dancing with her. He'd then tell the starry-eyed girl she should look him up when they reached the valley. However, the little sneak never told the poor girl he meant Heber Valley, not Salt Lake Valley! Within a few days of leaving Laramie, I noticed David and George began passing up smaller groups as dusk approached, hoping to find a larger group that would likely hold a dance. I didn't object, since I spent most of my days wishing I were in David's arms.

We spent a cloudy, cool Sunday with a large group of Saints. They held a makeshift testimony meeting, with people sitting on rocks, logs or blankets. It was wonderful to hear the speakers loudly proclaim their faith in God and that they were meant to settle with the Saints in Zion. For the most part, the travelers we met were happy and rarely complained about the rigors of the journey.

The Saints often talked about the soon-to-be completed transcontinental railroad. Several members told me some of their fellow Saints in the eastern states had decided to wait to come to Zion until the railroad was completed. Then these same members would testify of their burning desire to follow the counsel of the Lord and gather with the Saints as soon as possible. It was inspiring to me. No longer would I complain when my parents suggested we walk the two blocks to church rather than drive the car.

George had been somber for a couple days, and after we set up camp beneath a bleak Wyoming hill, I asked him what was bothering him. He didn't want to talk, but I kept pestering him until he said, "We're close. I can feel it."

"To what? Yes, Fort Bridger can't be much further."

"No, not that," he said hastily. "We're near where my brother Robert died."

I took his arm, and we walked to the top of the hill. Moonlight bathed endless stretches of prairie in a faint glow. A river flowed past us to the south.

"This has to be the river, based on how Robert's group described it."

"What happened to him?" I asked.

"He'd gone rabbit hunting to help feed the group, but he never returned at the end of the day," George said. "The group searched all night, and they built huge fires to guide him back, but he was never seen again. A man found Robert's hat in the river, and they figured he tried to swim across the river and drowned."

We sat in silence, staring down at the river. I saw a small boulder halfway down the hill, and I nudged George with my elbow. "Let's leave him a monument," I said.

George looked thoughtful, then nodded. "That would be nice," he said.

We hollered at David, and he helped us slowly push the boulder to the top of the hill. We dug a small hole, then pushed the stone into it, making sure it would never roll again. George pulled out a knife, and he spent the night on the hill carving words into the face of the stone. When morning came, David and I climbed back up the hill to find George sleeping next to the stone, which now read:

Robert Dalton
1842-1866
A Good Brother

Chapter Fourteen

We reached Fort Bridger, and I stayed outside with the women this time. We restocked our supplies and pushed on, feeling so close to home. We reached the Wasatch Mountains in mid-September, putting us within a few days of Charleston. We eventually reached the small trail leading to Heber, which seemed primitive after spending so much time on the larger trails. Within hours we were deep within the mountains, following the Provo River. For the first time in many weeks, there wasn't anyone within miles of us.

We selected a campsite near a large pine tree. After building a fire, George and David rigged up two crude fishing poles with some hooks and string they'd purchased at Fort Bridger. While they fished for our dinner, I tried to gather enough firewood to last through the night. I couldn't find anything small enough to carry until I noticed several sticks wedged against a big rock in the middle of the river. The rock was about 10 feet from shore, but there were three stones a few feet apart that formed an easy route to the rock—at least easy for anyone with coordination.

The water looked deep and was running swiftly, but I cautiously hopped across the rocks to the pile of sticks. David was downstream, and he called out, "Emma, what are you doing?"

"I'm gathering firewood the easy way," I shouted, and I soon had tossed the whole pile of sticks onto the bank. I leaped off the big rock to the next stone, but my foot slipped, and I plunged into the frigid river!

David had observed my poor coordination for weeks now, so he'd anticipated this. As my head bobbed to the surface, he was already running toward me. "Can you touch bottom?"

My feet bounced off some rocks, but I couldn't slow myself. I was being swept downstream. "Help me, David!" I screamed. "I can't stop!"

My head went under again. Then I lurched to a halt. My left ankle had wedged between the branches of a submerged tree! The current forced my head under the water, and my lungs began to burn. I was one breath away from drowning.

David thrashed through the water to my side. Then he moved underwater along the tree until he reached my ankle. He couldn't budge my foot against the current, so he put his arms around the tree trunk and pushed his feet against the branch that held me captive. The branch snapped off, and my leg came free! I surfaced and breathed deeply, filling my lungs with precious air. David put his arm around my waist and helped me swim to shore. He pulled me onto the bank, then gave me a worried hug. "Don't scare me like that!" he said angrily.

"I'm sorry," I said. "My feet just don't work sometimes."

George had heard our shouts, and he rushed to us. "Are you all right?" he asked. "What happened?"

"This is how Emma gathers firewood." He gave me a quick glare and then started back to camp. I shrugged my shoulders at George. I knew David was angry at me, but what could I say? Could I help it if my brain and my feet had different agendas?

George put his jacket around my shoulders as we walked back to camp. "You sure know how to keep us on our toes, don't you?" he said. "Poor David has fallen in love, but he's afraid you'll get us all killed before you two ever reach the altar!"

I was cold, but my blood boiled. "What altar? Did he really say that?" I knew David had taken a liking to me, but I didn't think he liked me that much.

"That's pretty much what he said," George said sheepishly, knowing he'd said too much.

"I can't marry David!" I said. "I don't belong here!" I would've kept ranting, but we saw David standing at the fire, peering intently into the trees. He motioned for us to be quiet. As we approached he said, "We've got company coming, and I doubt they'll be polite."

We joined David at the fire as two Indian men on horseback

rode into camp. They appeared to be a father and son. Brigham's plan to feed the Indians had helped keep the peace, but many Indians were still furious at having their hunting grounds fenced off and the valleys turned into towns. They took out their anger by raiding small camps and even killing a few settlers in outlying areas.

Each of our visitors carried a rifle, and we hoped to avoid being their next targets. The younger man indicated he spoke some English. "We heard a woman scream," the man said.

David gave me an irritated look. "The girl fell into the river, and I pulled her out," he said. "We're fine now."

The Indians spoke to each other in their native tongue. Then the younger one spoke again. "White men took our tribe's horses and killed two of my brothers. To pay for it, you two will die, and the girl will go with us."

I didn't want to be separated, and I certainly didn't want to be carried off by these two. "I won't leave them," I said firmly. "You'll have to take us all with you."

"We'll just kill you all," he said. He got off his horse and pointed the gun at us, directing us to the base of the pine tree. "Sit and be quiet. If you talk, you get shot."

The men began sifting through our packs, and we became increasingly frustrated. Why couldn't people just leave us alone? I could hear David's teeth grinding, and George held his head in his hands. We were so close to Charleston! George had told us we'd reach his family's farm by sundown the next day, but now the journey had been for naught. Maybe someone would find our bodies in a few days. I wanted to cry, but I didn't want to die sooner than necessary. Then a small voice whispered, *"Sing."*

Sing? Now? I couldn't imagine a worse time to sing. But the prompting came again, and I began a song we'd often sung with the Saints around their campfires.

Come, come ye Saints, no toil nor labor fear, but with joy wend your way.
Though hard to you this journey may appear, grace shall be as your day.
Tis better far for us to strive, our useless cares from us to drive.
Do this, and joy your hearts will swell. All is well. All is well.

The Indians turned to watch me, while David and George stared at me as if I were suicidal. I moved to the next verse before the Indians decided to silence me permanently.

"Why should we mourn or think our lot is hard? 'Tis not so; all is right.
Why should we think to earn a great reward, if we now shun the fight?
Gird up your loins; fresh courage take. Our God will never us forsake.
And soon we'll have this tale to tell. All is well. All is well.

I was sure hoping I'd live to tell this tale. The Indians stood transfixed by the song, and my emotions now surfaced. I'd sung this song hundreds of times, but now the words took on a personal meaning. I got to my feet and poured my whole soul into the final two verses.

We'll find the place which God for us prepared, far away in the West.
Where none shall come to hurt or make afraid, there the Saints will be blessed.
We'll make the air with music ring, shout praises to our God and King.
Above the rest these words we'll tell—All is well. All is well.

And should we die before our journey's through, happy day! All is well!
We then are free from toil and sorrow, too. With the just, we shall dwell!
But if our lives are spared again to see the Saints their rest obtain,
Oh how we'll make this chorus swell—All is well. All is well!

A calm feeling settled over the camp, and I sat down again. The Indians moved closer, staring at me. "Go ahead and kill us," I said. "I feel ready to meet my Savior. There's no reason to wait around."

The Indians talked rapidly between themselves, and the younger one looked upset as the older man spoke to him forcefully. Then the younger man said to us, "I am angry over the deaths of my brothers, but the Great Spirit is with you. My father says we would offend the Great Spirit by killing you. So you will live."

I felt such relief, but we soon discovered that their kindness was limited—they quickly left camp with our horses and supplies. "Not again!" George muttered. "Horses slip through our fingers like sand."

We were angry and discouraged, but glad to be alive. I apologized for the problems I'd caused, but the men weren't upset. "Emma, if you hadn't sung that song, we'd be dead under that tree," David said. "Don't worry about it."

We took the branches I'd retrieved from the river and built a small shelter beneath the pine tree. Then we each snuggled deep into the thick layer of pine needles that had fallen there. It was a very prickly blanket, but it kept us warm throughout the night.

Chapter Fifteen

The men had dropped their fishing poles along the river when I'd fallen in, so they were able to find them and catch some fish for our breakfast. Then we had no choice but to start hiking down the trail. David stayed by my side and helped me along, but I still hadn't forgiven him for the angry attitude he'd shown after rescuing me. I was also bothered by George's "altar" statement, so rather than discuss it I gave David the silent treatment. He soon got exasperated and moved several yards ahead of me. In retrospect, I see he had valid reasons to be perturbed. I'd endangered his life several times, encouraged romance then spurned any hint of it, and basically tortured him with unpredictable behavior for several weeks.

As we hiked, George stayed with me. "There are some isolated homesteads out here, so watch for smoke," he said. Looking in vain for smoke kept my mind off my aching legs, but after trudging on for a few more hours, I couldn't go any further. We lost sight of David as I sat down on a stump. "I'm sorry I got you into this mess," I said. "Your father could have used your help."

He stood quietly for a moment, then asked, "Have you completed the errand President Young mentioned in the letter?"

"Well, no. I found the information I needed, but I need to get back to my home for it to be worth anything."

"Then I'm not done with my assignment, so quit apologizing. Do you feel rested enough?" I nodded, and we continued down the trail.

A few moments later we heard David hollering our names. We broke into a run and saw David talking with a gentleman on horseback. As we approached, David said, "This is Brother Murray, and he lives down the road. He'll take one of us with him to get another horse. Who should go?"

A day earlier I would've loved to send George off, leaving David and I alone as we walked down the trail, but now there was little question who should go.

"David, you better go," George said. David glanced at me, then nodded before climbing behind Brother Murray and disappearing down the trail.

David soon returned on one horse, while leading another. I quickly got behind George on the other horse, knowing I'd missed my chance to apologize. We reached Heber just before sunset, and an hour later we turned onto the road to the Dalton farm. George and I dismounted, and David took our horse's reins. He'd agreed to take the horses back to Brother Murray first thing in the morning.

"I guess this is good-bye," David said. "Have a safe trip back home."

"I'm not sure when I'll be leaving," I said. "Maybe we'll see each other again."

We both were at a loss for words, and after a few seconds of us staring at the ground, George took my arm and steered me toward the house.

"Thanks for everything, David," George said. "You were a lifesaver, literally."

David smiled sadly, then turned the horses toward his home. I wanted to shout a cheerful "Thanks!" to him, but it stuck in my throat.

George and I walked swiftly to the house, knowing our appearance would cause quite a commotion. We knocked on the door, and Finity opened it slightly.

"Who is it?"

"Just a couple of strangers looking for shelter," George said.

Finity stuck his head out, then broke into a huge grin. "Hooray! They're back!"

He pulled us to him in a big hug. The other family members surrounded us, and we all talked excitedly for several minutes.

The family then settled on the porch and listened in awe as we told them about our adventures. They gasped as we described the men at Fort Bridger, and they got a bit angry as we described our exciting events in Denver.

"That fat Larry sounds just horrible!" Elizabeth cried. "I wish I could tie him up and kick him around!"

The mood turned somber as George told about carving Robert's stone. "That was sweet of you, son," Mary said. "I'm sure Robert knows what you did."

"I'm just glad you survived in one piece," Finity said. "I know the Lord was keeping a close eye on you."

"The Lord deserves the credit," George said, "but David does too. He hardly took his eyes off Emma the whole trip." I blushed and slugged him in the arm, causing everyone to laugh. It was great to be back. The family soon got ready for bed, but not before Mary and Elizabeth prepared a special warm bath for me. George had to settle for a quick dip in the stream.

Chapter Sixteen

I slept on blankets on Elizabeth's bedroom floor, but that wasn't why I had a hard time sleeping. I couldn't stop pondering how I'd return to my own time and family. I wondered if I'd stumbled through some sort of time portal at the cemetery, and I nearly decided to travel back to Springville. I felt impressed to stay put, though. During that restless night, I finally convinced myself I was meant to live out my life in the 1800s. Then I'd pass the information on to someone who could use it, but who? My grandparents wouldn't even be born until the 1940s! The whole concept of being trapped in time made my head hurt, and I gratefully drifted off to sleep.

I was worried that Elizabeth was still angry about the quarrel we'd had over David. My first day back I cautiously asked her, "Can we work things out? I'm sorry we fought about David."

"What are you talking about?"

"Don't you remember our fight before I left?"

"Oh, that's all in the past," she said. "You can have David—I'm in love with Frank now."

My eyes bugged out of my head. *Frank?* How did this girl keep finding boys?

She seemed to read my mind. "Dad had to hire someone when George left with you, so he hired Frank Giles, and I'm so glad he did!"

"Does he know you like him?"

"Not exactly, but he's barely 17, so I have plenty of time."

I couldn't help but laugh. "You're still only 12 years…"

She put her hand to my mouth. "Stop the lecture. This one is different. You'll see."

I shrugged and smiled. "Then I'm happy for you. I'm glad we're friends again."

"Of course we are," she said. "Just don't start getting ideas about Frank!"

Finity and Mary asked me the next day when I planned to return home, and I told them I wasn't sure. They knew I lived in Springville, so they expected me to ask for help getting down Provo Canyon.

"Would it be all right if I stayed with you a little while longer?" I asked. "I'll gladly help out with the chores and the cooking."

"You are welcome to stay as long as you like," Finity said. They glanced at each other, and something passed between them. Finity hesitantly said, "George has told us you and David became a bit fond of each other on the journey. Is that why you want to stay?"

I blinked hard, hardly believing what I'd heard. "I'm fond of David, but I don't belong here. I have a whole other life waiting for me."

They looked puzzled, so I felt I should do some explaining. I asked them to step into their bedroom. We shut the door, and they each sat on the edge of the bed. I stood before them and gave them an unsure smile.

"I haven't been completely honest with you," I said. "I really am Joseph Dalton's descendant, but there's more to it. I'm also your descendant and George's descendant." They stared blankly at me, not comprehending.

"What do you mean, Emma?" Mary asked. "We don't even have any grandchildren."

"I know, but you will," I said. "Let me explain. I was born and raised in the late 20th century in Springville, but somehow I was brought back to 1868. I found the information my family needs, and now I expect to return to my time, in whatever manner the Lord sees fit."

That explanation completely bombed. "Please quit teasing us," Finity said sharply. "We're glad you and David like each other, so stop the foolish talk. Now please excuse me. I've got horses to feed."

He started to get off the bed, but I jumped in front of him. "What I've told you is true," I said urgently. "Brigham Young himself knows it's true. When I found myself in the 1860s, you were the only relatives I was sure were living in Zion, so I came to you. Please believe me!"

He studied my face for a moment, then sat back down on the bed. I tried to think calmly, but I was so intent on convincing them that I threw out any sense of caution.

"You can be proud of your posterity," I said. "They have multiplied by the hundreds and have now spread throughout these valleys. You're my great-great-great-great-grandparents, and George is also one of my ancestors, which made the trip to Denver a little strange at first, but now he's like my brother. Anyway, in a few years, George will have a son named Robert, who will have a son named Keith, who will have a son named Jack, who will have a son named Mark, who is my father. Does that make sense?"

I knew it didn't. They'd never seen a pedigree chart in their lives. "I'm sorry. I shouldn't have said anything," I said. "Let's drop this for now." Finity nodded wearily, but Mary had an enlightened, understanding look in her eyes.

"So the Dalton name will carry on for generations to come?" she asked. "I find that very exciting! As you know, we've lost several children, and we've often worried whether any of our children would live to adulthood. It's wonderful to know they will!"

Finity finally caught a glimpse of what I was saying. "So you know when I die?" he asked. "I hope it isn't soon!"

I smiled. "Don't worry. I don't remember the exact dates, but you'll both live into the 1890s, and all of your remaining children will live far into the next century."

They were now eager to hear more. I felt a strong prompting to clamp my lips shut, but I was enjoying this too much. "The

1900s are filled with marvelous inventions I can barely begin to describe," I said. "We have horseless carriages called cars that travel at great speed. In my day, George and I would've been to Denver and back in two days. We drive these cars on smooth roadways that stretch from coast to coast."

Their eyes gleamed, and Mary exclaimed, "How wonderful! What else?"

"There's machines to wash your dishes and sew your clothes and tractors that harvest your grain for you," I said. "Despite hundreds of marvelous inventions, there will be two horrible world wars and a terrible economic crisis. But the church is growing rapidly and has reached nearly every nation. We have huge machines called airplanes that fly missionaries to every part of the world, and our country has even landed people on the moon!"

Oops! I'd gone too far. Serious doubt crept onto their faces. This time Finity rose off the bed with no intention of sitting back down.

"I wish what you're saying is true, but it sounds like a big fairy tale," he muttered. "You said President Young knows about this? I think I'll write him a letter and see what he says. It's General Conference time, so he ought to be in Salt Lake."

Finity was agitated enough by what I'd said that he sent off a letter that very day. I felt like a fool. I'd told them wonderful things about their family that they wanted to believe, but they couldn't help doubting the flying machines and moon missions. Thankfully, Finity and Mary chose not to tell the rest of the family about our conversation. I threw myself into the chores, trying to keep busy, and urgently praying that President Young would quickly reply.

I was in luck. Five days later Finity received a letter from the prophet. I watched as he and Mary read through the letter together. They didn't seem too overjoyed, but they did seem relieved by what the letter contained. Finity finally handed me the letter. It read:

Dear Finity,

Thank you very much for assisting Emma with her mission. I'm happy she has returned safely. As for what she has told you, it is all true. The Lord has shown me her day, and she has described it accurately. It has been made known to me that she is indeed from a future time, with an errand to fulfill among us.

In closing, please kindly remind Emma that I counseled her to keep her mouth firmly closed about the future! That counsel still stands.

Your brother in the gospel,

President Brigham Young

Finity had a small grin on his face as he watched me read the letter. I was stung by Brigham's rebuke, but I knew he was right. Finity put his arm across my shoulders and said, "I'm sorry I doubted you, and to be honest, I regret not getting more information out of you while I had the chance. But let's not talk about trips to the moon anymore, all right? No matter what, I'm proud of you, granddaughter."

I looked up into his eyes, happy that he had accepted me. I gave him a big hug, then Mary joined the hug, too. These truly were special people.

Chapter Seventeen

With few options, I stayed with the Daltons. Finity asked me to help out with the animals, and George led me to the barn. "Your main job is to milk Old Betsy each afternoon," he said.

"Can't I just gather eggs?"

He laughed. "Where's that spunkiness I saw when you outfoxed that fool Larry?"

"Oh, all right. I'll give it a try."

It took me nearly an hour to fill the bucket the first night, especially with the kids watching and laughing as I struggled to get any milk out of the cow's udders. But within a week I figured it out and could fill the bucket in minutes. George told Finity about my progress, and he came to watch me.

"George says you're quite a milkmaid," he said, "so I thought I'd see if you're using some special technique you'd learned in the future."

We both laughed. "Nope, I'm doing it the usual way, although in the future they use machines to milk hundreds of cows at the same time."

"Hold on!" he said in exasperation. "You're making me think too hard again!"

I milked the cow for a moment, listening to the milk splash into the bottom of the bucket. Then I said, "I forgot to tell you I met Joseph F. Smith in Provo this summer. He told me to tell you hello."

Finity got a gentle look in his eyes. "What a fine young man. Did you know that without him I'd still be plowing a tiny field in England? He's too modest to say it, but he's the whole reason I brought my family to Zion."

"What do you mean?" I asked. "George told me you joined the church many years ago."

"I did join the church in 1842, but we were too poor to come to America, and soon nearly all the Saints had left for Zion. Our neighbors had ridiculed us when we joined the church, and we took a lot of abuse over the years. After the Saints left, we still lived the gospel, but to ease the tension in the neighborhood, we stopped mentioning we were Mormons. I'm ashamed to admit I even returned to some of my old ways. I was more worried about what my neighbors thought than what the Savior thought."

He paused and rubbed his eyes. I'd never heard this story before, and I waited anxiously for him to continue. The stalwart Finity had once wavered in the faith? It shook me a little.

He finally cleared his throat and said, "Anyway, that's where Joseph F. comes into the picture. By 1863 I'd pretty much forgotten about Mormonism, but one day the plow blade broke and I had to go into town. As I entered the town square to find a blacksmith, I noticed two Americans preaching there, and one was a tall young man wearing a stovepipe hat. He was preaching the gospel of Jesus Christ and saying his uncle Joseph Smith had seen the Father and the Son. A crowd gathered around, and they viciously heckled poor Joseph F., but he stood his ground and kept right on preaching. Then a man brought out a bucket of rotten eggs and began to pelt the missionaries. I felt my Mormon loyalty return, and when the man knocked off Joseph F.'s hat with an egg, I couldn't take it anymore. I rushed at the man with the eggs and knocked his basket across the street, then shouted, 'These men speak the truth! Leave them alone!'

"I went to the missionaries and told them I was a Mormon. Then I led them back to my house. The incident rekindled my faith, and the whole family was baptized. We came to Zion the next year. It never would've happened if Joseph F. hadn't stood strong against that horrible crowd. I'm so grateful to him." He chuckled a little, then said, "I'm also grateful for that broken plow. You know, I never did get that blasted thing fixed!"

Two weeks passed, and David had visited me four times. He didn't say much—he'd just help me with my evening chores, and then we'd sit on the porch with the family and join in their conversations. I was so happy to be back on friendly terms with him, and the Daltons really liked him. Even Mary couldn't resist teasing me a little.

"David sure stops by a lot lately," she said with a twinkle in her eye. "Are you two getting along again?"

"Nothing's going on between us, " I said. "We haven't even held hands."

"Oh, you will soon enough," she said. "That boy is hooked."

I admitted to her I was ready to start courting seriously, and she thought it was a good idea. So I started encouraging him with coy smiles, and it paid off. An "End of the Harvest Dance" was planned in Heber on Friday evening, and David asked me to accompany him. But he had one request.

"Do you promise you won't throw your body into contortions like you did at that campfire dance?" David asked. "My friends will be there."

I blushed. "I promise. I don't know what came over me that night."

"We didn't either," he said seriously. "We were going to give you a blessing, but when you acted normal again the next morning, we figured it must've been something you ate."

Mary loaned me one of her nicest dresses, and I anticipated a memorable night. David picked me up in his family's wagon, and the evening started off well. We sat close together on the wagonseat as we traveled to Heber, holding hands and teasing each other. An unforeseen problem arose when we arrived at the dance, though. Many of Heber's young men wanted to share company with "the new girl in town," and they sometimes would cut in on us during a dance, forcing David out of the way. But David danced with me as much as possible, each time asking me why I was dancing with those "city boys." I kept telling him I didn't have a choice. As the dance went on, I saw David's patience wearing thin, and finally I told him to take me home.

It was a quiet ride back to the farm. David walked me to the door out of pure courtesy, but he was still fuming. I didn't want to end the night on a sour note, so I opened the door and told Mary that we were back, but that we'd be chatting outside for a few minutes. We then walked around the house and stood together against the barn.

"Emma, I'm sorry I let those city boys bother me," he said. "But I have tender feelings for you, and I couldn't help but get jealous. I mean, that was my future wife out there."

I stiffened. His wife?

"I'm fond of you, but let's not talk about marriage yet," I said. "Don't forget I still have to take that information to my family. I might be leaving soon."

He threw his hands into the air in exasperation. "We've been back from Denver for three weeks now, and you're still here! If you need to travel to Springville, I'll gladly take you there. I'd like to meet your family."

"No, that won't work."

"What do you mean?" he asked. "I hope to someday ask for your hand in marriage, and your father will surely have something to say about that. Why must I wait before I meet them?"

I stood there against the barn, unable to think of a reply. Then David placed his right hand under my chin and brought his lips down on mine. A flame of adrenaline shot through my whole body. I pulled back a moment. Then I put my arms around his neck and gave him a kiss he'd never forget! We held each other tight, looked deep into each other's eyes, then kissed again.

As wonderful as it was, the rush of love I felt was quickly overpowered by sadness. I knew this wasn't our destiny, and I'd shatter David's heart. "We can't be together," I cried. "This isn't meant to be!"

I broke free from him and rushed into the pitch-black barn. I had to get away from him, or I might find myself too much in love to ever leave. I quickly climbed into the hayloft and watched from above as David entered the barn. He called out my name. Then he saw the straw tumbling down between the slats in the loft.

"Quit playing games," he said. "Come down, or I'll have to

find you!" I stayed silent, and he began climbing into the loft. I started working my way to a ladder on the other side of the loft, but it was too dark to see anything, and the footing was treacherous. I nearly fell through twice, but I kept moving.

I reached the ladder and got a foot on it, but the ladder twisted, and I had nothing to grab! I screamed, then toppled to the hard-packed floor, landing hard on my left shoulder and head. The pain was unbearable, and I began to black out. Just before I lost consciousness, I heard David shout from the loft, "Emma, please be all right! I love you!" Those tender words were the last thing I heard during my journey to 1868, and they haunted me for months.

Chapter Eighteen

When I awakened from the fall, I nearly drowned! I found myself submerged in very cold water. I was beginning to hate cold water! I paddled furiously upward, and when my head popped to the surface, I found myself in a big lake. The shore was about 50 yards away, and I swam as hard as I could. I soon touched bottom, and I trudged through mud to the shore, falling to the ground and shivering terribly.

Where was David? Where was I? Then it dawned on me. I was back! That graceless tumble out of the hayloft was what it took to send me back to my own time! I looked across the water, and this was undoubtedly Deer Creek Reservoir. The Dalton farm had been covered up by the reservoir in the 1920s, so when I returned, I logically ended up in the lake.

It felt like late autumn because the back of Mount Timpanogos was covered with snow, and the reservoir was certainly too cold for water-skiing. I stood up, but the dress I was wearing was soaked and weighed me down. I pulled it off, leaving me in 1860s-style women's underwear, which was actually more modest than some modern-day outerwear. This underwear was so thick that it wasn't even see-through when wet.

I studied the hills to the south where the highway should be, and sure enough, I saw a pair of headlights come around a bend. I was elated to be back, but I could tell I was starting to enter the first stages of hypothermia. Plus, my injured shoulder and neck were starting to throb.

I stumbled my way to the highway, hoping to flag down a passing motorist. I leaned on the guardrail, holding my thumb out. Several cars passed by me, and one even honked. I probably looked like a ghost in that old-time underwear. I felt myself getting weaker and weaker, and then I slumped over the railing and closed my eyes.

A few minutes later I heard a car stop next to me. I raised my head to see a Utah Highway Patrol car. The car's lights were flashing, and I weakly waved my arm. The officer jumped out of the car. "Miss, what in the world happened to you?" he asked.

"You wouldn't believe me, so don't ask."

He lifted me off the guardrail and carried me to the car. "We need to get you to a hospital," he said. "You're as cold as ice."

The police officer gently placed me in the car's passenger seat and strapped on my seatbelt. He got behind the wheel, flipped on the siren and roared down Provo Canyon to Utah Valley Medical Center. I slipped in and out of consciousness during the ride, but I remember the officer talking about his four-year-old daughter. He told me that every time he rescued a young girl, he prayed his daughter would stay out of trouble as she grew older.

I jerked awake as the car screeched to a stop at the emergency room entrance. The officer had radioed ahead, and two nurses waited with a stretcher. The officer helped them transfer me to the stretcher, and I touched his arm, thanking him for saving me.

"I always stop when I see a girl hanging over a highway guardrail," he said with a smile. "I was just doing my job." He then entered the hospital to fill out a report.

The nurses rushed me into the emergency room and did a great job warming me up. They took off that old-fashioned underwear and put me in some warm clothes. Then they examined me for injuries. I heard one of them mention that other than a deep shoulder bruise, the only other sign of injury was some healing saddle sores. Then they let me lie down and rest.

One of the nurses waited until the other left the room. Then she came to my side. "Where did you get that nifty underwear?" she asked. "Is this Calvin Klein's newest gimmick?" I was too tired to laugh. I stayed silent, content to never move again.

I was gently awakened by the patrol officer who had saved me. "I never introduced myself. I'm Officer Jeremy Cobb," he said. "I'm helping to register you, and we have a slight problem. We don't know your name!"

I laughed, realizing that I had no identification on me at all. "I'm sorry, I should've told you earlier. I'm Emma Dalton."

You would've thought I'd announced I was Amelia Earhart! Officer Cobb stared at me in amazement for a moment, then said, "You *are* Emma Dalton!" He ran out of the room, and soon my bed was surrounded by two doctors, two nurses and three police officers.

"We've called your parents and they're on their way," a nurse said. As I listened to the conversations around me, the enormity of what had happened sunk in. I noticed a calendar on the wall, and it showed the month of October! Time had rolled along here at the same speed as it had in 1868. I had vanished off the face of modern-day earth for three months! My poor parents! They must've gone crazy with worry when I never returned from Leah's funeral.

The officers began asking me questions, and I decided to be as vague as possible.

"Emma, where have you been? Were you kidnapped?"

"I was taken to Denver by two men. They brought me back a few weeks later."

"Why didn't you contact anyone?"

"Well, I never saw a phone, and I never talked with anyone who could've helped me contact the proper authorities."

"Then how did these men transport you? Surely they stopped at a gas station where you could've signaled someone."

"No, we traveled to Denver and back on horses. After our return, one of the men chased me into Deer Creek Reservoir, where Officer Cobb found me."

"That's a strange twist. Did they ever assault you in any way?"

"No. They were perfect gentlemen for the most part, although the older one did hurt my feelings a few times."

"Can you describe them?"

"Certainly." I then gave the officers a perfect description of both George and David, along with their first names. I later saw the police artist's sketches of them on the news, and they were nearly perfect matches! Not that they'd ever find them.

The police officers asked me a few more questions, then we heard a commotion in the hall. My parents and Doug burst into the room. Their faces were tear-stained, and I couldn't help bawling myself. They embraced and kissed me again and again. During my journey, I had purposely suppressed how much I'd missed them, and now all that pent-up emotion came pouring out. There soon wasn't a dry eye in the room.

Outside the room, someone shouted, "Emma, you're on TV!" They turned on the room's television, and KSL's anchorman was talking about me, with "Special Report" across the bottom of the screen. My senior yearbook picture was in the upper corner. The anchorman then turned the story over to a reporter standing outside the hospital. His report was pretty accurate, even down to the two men taking me to and from Denver on horseback and chasing me into the reservoir.

For the next 10 minutes we turned to each local station and watched them give their reports on my return. This whole circus atmosphere was starting to make me a bit uncomfortable. I would've preferred being fought over again by David and Heber's "city boys" than endure much more of this.

"Why do all these people even care who I am, Mom?"

"We were in a panic for weeks when you never returned home," she said. "We've searched everywhere for you, and the media has latched onto your story. It's not everyday a teenage girl vanishes after a funeral. Plus, it was Doug Dalton's sister missing, so it added to the local interest. Nearly everyone in Utah knows your name by now. Several relatives have banded together and offered a $5,000 reward to whoever helped you return safely."

"That's good to hear," I said. "I want Officer Cobb to have the reward. Several cars passed me on the road tonight, but he was the only one who stopped. I would've frozen to death without him. He deserves it."

I was able to return home the next day, and I was so happy! There were some adjustments those first few days, such as wiggling into blue jeans again—they felt so confining after wearing only dresses for three months. I had little trouble getting back behind the wheel of the family car, although 60 miles per hour felt way too fast after plodding along on those trails.

It was great to see Doug again. After my return, I noticed he'd inherited Finity's smile, and it was a constant reminder of my journey. We spent a lot of time together, and we grew closer than ever. My disappearance had really bothered him, and he had carried around a lot of worry and despair. It had even affected his performance on the football field. But soon things were back to normal, and we had a good time teasing Mom that she now had enough newspaper clippings about us to keep her busy with scrapbooks for a long time.

We also had to juggle reporters' calls and TV interviews. The media couldn't get enough of my story. Besides being a "feel good" story, they loved the angle of the horseback ride to Denver, and I soon regretted ever mentioning it. The TV interviews almost always began, "Emma, this kidnapping sounds like something out of the 1800s..." They had no idea how right they were.

I spoke by satellite with all of the TV networks, besides traveling to Salt Lake to do interviews with the local stations. It was exciting, but after a few days, I was old news. The president got embroiled in another big scandal; a woman gave birth to six babies in Idaho, and a strong earthquake shook the Northwest. The media chased after those stories, and my 15 minutes of fame quickly ended. A search was launched for my "kidnappers," but after a few weeks my case was filed away with other unsolved crimes.

After my final TV interview in Salt Lake, I'd wandered over to Temple Square, admiring the beautiful flowers. I gazed up at the Salt Lake Temple and remembered Brigham's vow to complete it. He didn't live to see it finished, but I'm sure he's pleased with the finished product.

I soon crossed the street and entered the Joseph Smith Memorial Building to see the film "Legacy," a story of the early years of the Saints and their journey to the Salt Lake Valley. I'd seen the film once with a youth group, but now it took on a deeper meaning. As I sat in the darkened theater watching the

Saints struggle for the gospel's sake, my journey came alive again. I had been there! I had mingled with these people who worked so hard to build Zion.

The family in the film had a son named Johnny. He reminded me so much of George, even down to the clothes he wore. When Johnny was killed by a mob at Haun's Mill, it pierced my soul. Then the new convert David came onto the scene, and I was mesmerized. His kindness and playful ways reminded me so much of my David! I sobbed, not necessarily in sorrow, but in grief at being separated by more than a century from the man I loved. Every time David was mentioned, I felt torn apart. What a brutal coincidence! I knew the film's main character, Eliza, would marry her David, but mine was forever beyond my grasp. I finally couldn't take it anymore, and I rushed out of the theater. The missionary sisters at the door tried to stop me, but I shoved past them. I was feeling really shaky, and I needed to talk to somebody about my journey.

I found my car and headed straight home. So far I'd followed President Young's counsel to keep my mouth shut, but surely he only meant in the 1860s. Either way, I was ready to crack—I couldn't keep it bottled up inside much longer. My parents deserved to know the whole story, but Finity and Mary hadn't believed me at first. Would my parents find the story any more believable? Then I thought of young Joseph Smith, who, after seeing the Angel Moroni, had confided in his father. I hadn't seen an angel, but that was almost more believable than my story. But Joseph's father had believed him, and I decided to confide in my parents.

I pulled into our driveway just as Dad was leaving for a church meeting. He saw my tear-splattered face and rushed to the car. "What's wrong, honey? Are you OK?"

"No, I'm not. I know you've got a meeting, but I really need to talk with you and Mom."

"That's fine," he said. "Let me make a phone call and get your mom."

"We need to go somewhere private, Dad, with no chance of being interrupted."

I could tell he was getting really worried, and I could see every possible "teenage daughter" problem running through his head. His eyes got big, and I touched his arm to comfort him. "It's nothing to worry about, Dad," I said with a laugh. "Just get Mom and we'll go up the canyon."

We drove up Hobble Creek Canyon to the Kelly's Grove picnic area. We sat at a table under a secluded pavilion, and I told them the whole story, even the smooching I did with David.

"Whew, it could've been worse," Dad said.

"So you believe me?"

"Of course!" they said in unison.

"Oh, I'm so glad! It's been so hard to keep that inside."

"I knew you couldn't really be gone from our lives," Dad said. "I'd look into your bedroom, and everything was still as you'd left it the morning of Leah's funeral. I sensed you'd return. You're a talented girl, and you've completed a special mission."

"This has been traumatic for our family," Mom said, "but it sounds like your experience is an answer to our prayers about our genealogy. I just wish there had been an easier way!"

They asked me to repeat the family information Esther had told me, and they nodded happily. "Esther sounds like a special person," Dad said. "We need to get working on this right away. To you, it seems like only a few weeks since you talked to her, but it's really been more than 130 years! I'd imagine those ancestors are getting antsy to have their temple work done."

We agreed to start doing the research the following Saturday, but I couldn't wait that long to see if my adventures had been recorded by the people I'd known in 1868. I didn't even bother checking Brigham Young's writings—he never would have written about me. I searched through all the Dalton histories, but apparently I was just a blip on the radar screen of their lives, not worth even a sentence. I was sad that neither Finity nor Mary had written anything about their lives. What would Finity have written about me anyway? *"We housed a girl from the future in the summer of 1868…"* No way.

George's history was puzzling because he did mention

traveling to Denver as a teenager, and he even talked about carving Robert's stone, but he never mentioned the people he'd traveled with. Arghh! So close. Maybe I'd put poor George through enough headaches that he preferred to forget me.

I even drove to the little Charleston Cemetery and found the headstones of the Daltons. Finity, Mary, and George were all there. Nearby was a headstone for Frank Giles and his wife Elizabeth Dalton Giles. All right! She'd finally gotten her man. I couldn't find the name I was really looking for, though. I looked twice at every headstone in that cemetery before I finally accepted that David wasn't buried there. He must've eventually moved from Charleston.

While I was in the area I took a walk along Deer Creek Reservoir's eastern shore. I found the spot where I'd climbed out of the water, and I was surprised to find Mary's dress right where I'd left it. I checked the front pocket, and sure enough, there was the wooden horse John had carved for me. I'd carried the horse as a good-luck charm, and I'm glad it had survived the trip. It now rests on my bedroom dresser.

The dress was frozen and crumpled, but I took it home, where I washed and ironed it. The dress now hangs in my closet. It's a nice keepsake from my journey, although I feel guilty about never returning one of Mary's nicest dresses. I suppose she has gotten over it by now. I never did bother tracking down my old-time underwear, although I suspect a certain nurse wears it when she wants to feel stylish!

As I drove back down Provo Canyon, I couldn't resist stopping at Bridal Veil Falls. I was pleased to see that a better trail was in place than when I'd stumbled across the rocks with the Johnson boys. I hiked to the bottom of the falls, which had hardly changed. I looked in amazement at where I'd stood under that thundering cascade. Had I been out of my mind? It shows where a little peer pressure can take you. The area is now off-limits, and wisely so.

After the cemetery visit, I tried to put David out of my thoughts, but I was still very infatuated with a man who'd probably been dead for 70 years. He'd been in my thoughts daily since I left him in that barn. I suppose he climbed down from that hayloft to find, well, nothing! There probably was a mark on the barn floor where I'd hit, but it must have been a huge shock to him when he couldn't find me anywhere. I hoped he'd dealt with it all right.

With the excuse that I just wanted to make sure David had moved on with life, I went to Springville's Family History Library and sat down at a computer. My fingers trembled as I called up the Ancestral File and typed in David's name. A list of several David Norths came on the screen, so I selected the one born in 1849. Within moments, I read the following information:

North, David	Born: 8 Jan 1849	Place: Salt Lake, Salt Lake, Utah
	Died: 6 Sep 1922	Place: Heber, Wasatch, Utah
	Married: 3 Aug 1874	Place: Endowment House, SLC, Utah
	Spouse:	Judy Bartholomew

I was stunned. He'd actually gotten married! So what if he'd waited nearly six years after I'd disappeared? I felt discarded.

"That two-timing jerk!" I muttered, banging my fist on the desk. The library supervisor came to my side and studied the computer screen.

"What seems to be the problem?" she asked.

I bit back a sarcastic remark and instead said, "I'm sorry to cause a scene. I've done a lot of research on this man, and I've just found out he's had all his work done." Including his sealing to a spouse, I thought bitterly.

"Maybe you should've checked this file before you got started," she said kindly. I nodded, trying to get rid of her.

"I'll be sure to do that next time," I said. "Thanks for your help."

She gave me an unsure smile, then left me in my misery. My mind told me I was being stupid, but my heart was aching. I don't know if I'd secretly hoped we'd get married in the next life or what, but it didn't matter now.

Out of curiosity, I called up David's family group sheet. David and Judy only had two children, a boy and a girl. The daughter died at age eight, but the son apparently lived to adulthood. There wasn't any further information on him. I shut down the computer and went home. "Well, at least I can stop worrying about that," I said to myself.

Chapter Nineteen

On Saturday my parents and I traveled to the LDS Family History Library across the street from Temple Square, where we had one of the greatest days of our lives. By using the information Esther had shared with me, we struck a genealogical bonanza! We had little trouble finding Thomas and Sarah Cooper in Bristol, and then we followed the family's path back to Manchester. It was wonderfully exciting, like finding long-lost friends. We also found a book on the shelf that listed thousands of Coopers in England, and we were able to tie some of those people into our family tree.

We were especially exuberant when Dad discovered another book that mentioned dozens of Sarah's ancestors. Our hearts burned with conviction that these people had accepted the gospel and were eagerly waiting for us to perform their temple ordinances.

We copied the information down and soon processed the names through the church's Temple Ready program. We were surprised to find that much of the temple work had already been completed through the church's extraction program or by church members who were distantly related to us. But that still left us with hundreds of ancestors who hadn't received their temple ordinances. We decided to submit the vast majority directly to the temple for other temple visitors to do, but we set aside several of our closest ancestors so we could perform their temple ordinances ourselves.

One exciting thing we discovered was that Henry and Esther Sheridan had never been sealed to each other. I did a little research, and I found out the Sheridans did indeed settle down in a small Colorado town and open up a hotel. They also had several children who'd never been sealed to them. So Mom and Dad made that their first priority on their next trip to the temple. They were sealed for eternity in behalf of Henry and Esther, and then the children were sealed to their parents. My parents said there was a heavenly feeling in the room during the ordinance.

Nobody had played a bigger role than Esther in helping us discover those names, and it fills me with joy to know their family is now progressing together toward eternal life.

Since I hadn't yet been through the temple for my own endowments, the only ordinances I would perform in behalf of my deceased relatives were the baptisms and confirmations for the women. Doug would be baptized and confirmed for the men, and our parents would take care of the other ordinances.

Doug and I planned to go to the temple together on a Tuesday afternoon, but I woke up that morning at 5:30 a.m. with an urgent desire to go that very moment. I told my parents where I was going, then drove alone to the Provo Temple to be baptized for 20 of my ancestors. I changed into white clothing and waited my turn on a bench near the baptismal font as other people were baptized. Finally it was my turn. I walked down into the font, but the man who'd been doing the baptizing climbed up the steps. A good-looking younger man stepped out of the dressing room and came into the font. He appeared to be in his early 20s, and as he took my wrist, he smiled at me and said, "Hi, I'm Tad. Have you done this before?"

I nodded, and he began baptizing me. I pondered Tad's question. His smile, blue eyes and sandy-brown hair seemed so familiar. Maybe we *had* done this before. Was this guy a senior in high school when I was a sophomore? I was so busy trying to figure out who he was that the baptisms were over before I hardly knew it. Tad took my arm and helped me out of the font. As he went back down into the water, I turned around and stared at him. The next girl to be baptized elbowed her way past me, and Tad looked up at me. "I noticed those were family names," he said. "Did I pronounce them correctly?"

"Yes, you did fine. That's not what's bothering me. Don't I know you?"

"I don't think so," he said. "Thanks for coming to the temple." Then he turned his attention to the girl in the font. I could've stood there and stared at him for another 10 minutes on his good looks alone, but the attendant finally grabbed my arm and guided me to the women's dressing room. I dried off and quickly changed into my dress, hoping I could talk with Tad. I entered the baptismal foyer, but he was still performing baptisms. I then waited in a booth for my confirmations to be performed, and there was a long wait. At least 45 minutes passed before I returned to the lobby. Tad wasn't in the font anymore! I went up to the clerk at the main desk and asked, "Do you have a record of who performs the baptisms? I'd like to know the name of the man who baptized me."

The clerk at the desk shuffled through his papers. "Now who was it? The older man with gray hair or the young man with brownish hair?"

"The young man."

"Let's see. His name is Tad North."

The name rattled me as if I'd been struck with a plank. Tad North! Could he be a descendant of David? What were the chances of that? No, that would be too strange, but what about that smile and those eyes?

"Has he left yet?" I nearly shouted.

"Shh, please keep your voice down in the temple. Yes, he left about five minutes ago."

I bounded up the stairs, waited impatiently for the temple's automatic glass doors to open, then rushed into the parking lot. There he was! He was getting into an older blue Honda near the west gate. I shouted at him and ran down the sidewalk, but he backed out and drove away before I could catch his attention.

I stopped on the sidewalk, out of breath, but happy. "Tad, you're not getting away from me that easily."

The determination I'd felt in the temple parking lot had ebbed considerably that evening as I sat in my bedroom with my phone in one hand and the phone book in the other. I'd courageously started out by dialing a random North family in Provo. The girl who answered the phone turned out to be Tad's cousin, and she happily gave me Tad's number. She said Tad had grown up in St. George, but he was currently living in a Provo apartment. I carefully pumped the girl for some information, and I discovered Tad had returned from a mission to Australia five months earlier, and he was now a sophomore at BYU.

Everything sounded good so far, except now I was extremely nervous. I dialed six of the seven digits in his phone number 10 times before hanging up each time. Finally I said, "This is it. Call him now or forever hold your peace."

I dialed and let it ring. A man answered the phone and I blurted out, "Hi, are you Tad?"

"No, but hold on. He's right here."

I began to sweat profusely. What do I say now?

"Hello, this is Tad."

"Hi, Tad. This is Emma Dalton. Have you ever heard of me?" What a stupid thing to say.

"I don't think so," he said. "Should I have?"

That was a mark against him right off the bat. He obviously didn't watch the news or read the newspaper.

"I guess there's no reason you should know me," I said. "Remember the girl you baptized this morning who stared at you for a while?"

"Oh yeah! With the light brown hair and blue eyes. What was going on with you this morning? I was worried my pants were unbuttoned or something."

"I just thought I knew you," I said. "I guess I still feel that way. Would you mind if we got together for lunch or something?" Wow! That's the last thing I'd planned on saying.

"That would be fine. Are you going to BYU?"

"Not right now. I skipped this semester for family reasons, but I'll be starting classes in January."

"That's cool," he said. "Well, I've got a class in the Tanner Building that gets out at 10:50 tomorrow morning. Then I've got a class at noon in the Harris Fine Arts Center. Why don't we meet at the CougarEat at 11? Will that work for you?"

"Sounds great!"

"Thanks for giving me a call. I'll see you tomorrow!"

I took a shower to rinse off the buckets of sweat I'd generated talking to Tad, then settled into bed for a long, sleepless night.

Chapter Twenty

As Tad walked toward me in the CougarEat, he looked even better than I'd remembered. We greeted each other, then went inside and found an empty table. I tried to be casual and not too bubbly, and it must've worked because Tad and I hit it off really well during that lunch. But time flew by, and all too soon he had to leave for his next class.

"Well, it was nice talking with you," I said. "Maybe I'll see you around campus next semester."

"Yeah, that would be great," he said. "By the way, I've got to be in Springville Friday afternoon. Maybe I could stop by and give you a visit. Would you mind giving me your address and phone number?"

"That would be fine," I said, reaching into my purse for paper and a pen. As I wrote down my address, I asked, "Why do you have to go to Springville?"

My question seemed to take him by surprise, and he stammered, "Um, I have to deliver a few things to a friend." He stopped, and I noticed he was blushing.

"Oh, who am I kidding?" he said. "I'm trying to be Mr. Cool, but I'm failing miserably, so I'll just get to the point. I don't have any reason to go to Springville, except to see you. Will you go out with me Friday night?"

"That sounds fun. I think I can work it into my schedule." I handed him my address.

"Great! I'll pick you up at seven. See you then!"

He headed off to class, and I wandered around campus for a while, unable to keep a big grin off my face. Yes! He had asked me out! I even jumped into the air and clicked my heels without falling clumsily to the ground. The sun had never shined brighter on my world.

Tad's roommates obviously followed the news more closely than he did, because by Friday night they'd filled him in about my "kidnapping." We went to Trafalga in Orem for a round of miniature golf, and while we played he asked a lot of questions about my story, including the main question I was always asked.

"Why didn't you just jump off the horse and run into the woods?"

I gave him my standard answer. "These were nice guys, but they always kept a gun handy. I didn't want to risk it." He seemed to accept that.

Toward the end of our golf round I casually asked Tad if any of his North ancestors had been named David. He gave me a funny look. "I have no idea," he said. "I've never worried about that stuff."

"I was just curious," I said. "I know a few Norths that live near Heber, and you look a lot like them."

"It seems that some of my ancestors came from there," he said, "but we all live in Utah County or St. George now." He turned away to putt his ball. We dropped the subject, but it gave me a glimmer of hope. Now I'd just have to wait for the right opportunity to confirm my suspicions that Tad and David were related.

We spent a lot of time together over Christmas break, and I met his parents when they came up from St. George. They took us to a BYU basketball game, and I felt very comfortable around them. I couldn't help but think they'd be good in-laws.

Tad and I arranged to share a biology class once the winter semester started, and we continued to meet for lunch. Tad worked each afternoon as a professor's assistant, recording test scores and assignments. I stopped by to see him a lot, and I'd read him the scores as he marked them down. I loved being with him, and we became good friends. However, he apparently felt since we saw each other so much, we no longer needed to date.

I got fed up with being his "buddy," and while I should've quit visiting him at work to send him a message, I just couldn't resist being with him. It went on this way for a few weeks. Then one day as we walked out of biology class into the crowded hallway, he asked if I wanted to go bowling that night.

"Is this a date, or are we just going as pals?" I asked.

"Well, I don't know," he said. "I guess just as friends. Isn't that what you want?"

I felt like punching him. "This is what I want," I said. I grabbed his head and planted a solid kiss on his lips. I ignored the claps and whistles of other students and stormed out to my car. Not surprisingly, Tad called me that night. We started going on real dates again, but I still wondered if it would lead anywhere.

Tad is a basketball fan, and when he discovered Doug was a top-notch high school player, he attended all the games with us. It was nice to sit with someone besides my parents, and Tad and Dad really got along great. Plus, taking Tad to the game helped keep Mom under control. She is competitive by nature, and if one of Doug's games is close, she gets quite tense and obnoxious in the stands. With Tad attending the games, Mom was now on her best behavior to avoid scaring off my first boyfriend. Our fellow fans also appreciated Tad's attendance, because now they could watch the game in relative peace.

But during a close game against Provo High, Mom just couldn't restrain herself. At a quiet moment of the game, she stood and shouted, "Ref, you're as blind as a bat! That last call was horrible! Get off the floor right now!"

The whole crowd laughed, and Mom was mortified. She glanced over at Tad, hoping she hadn't cost me a boyfriend, but he was laughing. He reached over, patted her on the knee and said, "I couldn't have said it better myself."

I remember that night for a different reason, though. After the game, we sat in Tad's car outside my house for a while. As I was about to go inside, he grabbed my hand and said, "Emma, I really love your family. Your Dad is great, your Mom is a riot, and Doug is a neat kid. But what I love most about your family is you."

"Thanks, Tad. Yeah, my family is great. See you tomorrow."

"Emma, you missed what I said. I love you! You are the most wonderful girl I've ever met!" Then he kissed me, and I thought my heart would burst with joy.

"I love you too, Tad. I've loved you from first sight."

A week later we visited Tad's grandfather Charles North in Orem. While I was there, I told Charles I was interested in genealogy, and I asked him if I could look at his family pedigree charts. Tad looked at me as if I were crazy, and he quickly said, "Grandpa, while you and Emma paw through those dusty pages, I'll go water your tomatoes." That was fine with me! Now I could check out my hunch that Tad was related to David.

Charles brought out a few books from a back bedroom, and we sat down together on the couch. I eagerly opened his Book of Remembrance, and on the first page was a four-generation pedigree chart with pictures of each of his ancestors. I followed the top line with my finger and came across my beloved David, although he was at least 60 years old in the picture. I was glad to see he'd aged well.

I pointed at the picture. "Tad sure does look like David, doesn't he?"

"He really does," Charles said. "David was my great-grandpa, and he died just before I was born. My father told me David was a wonderful, caring man with a good sense of humor. Tad inherited those qualities, too."

"I know," I said. "Tad's everything I've ever hoped for. I think marriage is on our minds, but maybe we should wait awhile. It all seems so sudden."

"It's interesting you'd say that," Charles said. "I doubt Tad would think you should wait. Nearly all of the North boys married fairly young. I think David himself was the oldest to marry. Ironically, it was his advice that has prompted his descendants to not delay marriage once they've found their true love."

"What was David's advice?"

"He told his son and grandsons, 'Once you've found the girl of your dreams, don't let her slip through your fingers.'"

Charles was looking at the book as he said it, so he failed to see all the blood drain out of my face. I stumbled to my feet and said, "Thanks for letting me see these books. David sounds like an interesting guy."

"You're leaving so soon?" Charles asked. "We hardly got started!"

"Don't worry, I'll be back," I said. "I'm suddenly feeling a little queasy." I walked outside to see Tad finishing up in the garden. He saw me and called out, "Are you done already?"

"Yes, we'd better get going." I said good-bye to Charles, promising to return soon. As we drove to my house, Tad rambled on about improvements Charles' yard needed. I didn't mind letting him talk, because I was feeling lightheaded after seeing David's picture and verifying Tad was his descendant. The picture had forcefully reminded me of my journey, and after putting the trip out of my mind for several weeks, it all came rushing back. As Tad dropped me off at my house, he said, "Let's go out tonight. I've got something special to show you."

"Uh, sure. That's fine." I gave him a peck on the cheek, then I went straight to my room and collapsed on the bed with a pounding headache.

After the visit with Charles, I knew I needed to tell Tad the whole truth about my experience. Telling him might backfire, but it was a big part of my life, and as the visit had confirmed, it was also part of his life. The advice David had passed on to his family also bothered me. Charles treated it as symbolic, but I felt it was literal. I'd slipped away from David and broken his heart.

Seeing David's picture had changed me, though, and I could now let him go. He'd lived a good life, raised a family, and was now living happily in the spirit world. Maybe he'd even played "celestial matchmaker" for Tad and me. I now knew Tad was my true love.

When Tad picked me up that night, he acted aloof and nervous. My nerves hadn't completely settled either, so we were quite a jittery pair! We drove to Provo, and Tad soon pulled into the parking lot east of the Brick Oven Restaurant in Provo. I was surprised, because we rarely went on dinner-dates. Tad didn't earn a lot of money, but maybe Charles had slipped him some cash during our visit. We got out of the car, but instead of heading to the restaurant, Tad took my hand and guided me toward the stairs leading to the BYU campus.

"Where are we going?" I asked. "Aren't you hungry?"

"Not really," he said. "Why don't we go for a little walk?"

I didn't mind—food could wait. I was just happy to be with Tad. My surprise kiss after biology class had revved up the romance, and we'd fallen more in love each day since. We climbed the stairs and soon found ourselves at the back steps of the Maeser Building. I playfully hid behind a pillar, but Tad still seemed nervous. He sat on the top step and asked me to join him.

"What's wrong?" I asked. "You don't seem yourself tonight."

Tad slipped to one knee on the step below me and pulled a small box from his jacket. I gasped, not quite prepared for this moment.

"Emma, we've only known each other a few months, but I want to spend eternity with you. Will you marry me?"

I sat in silence, intending to say "Yes!" but unable to say the word. I had another topic on my mind. He nervously slipped the ring onto my finger anyway, and I admired it with a smile.

"We don't have to get married right away," he quickly added. "We can certainly wait a few months."

"It's not that," I said. "Yes, I'll marry you, on the condition you accept what I'm about to say. Remember me telling you about my kidnapping last summer?"

"Yes, of course."

"Well, there's more to that story than anyone knows, except my parents. They know the whole story, and if we're going to be together for eternity, you need to know everything, too. Are you willing to listen?"

"Certainly."

"It's getting cold on these steps, and this could take awhile," I said. "Why don't we take a walk through campus, then head back to the car?"

As we held hands, I told him my story. We walked through the nearly deserted campus, past the Kimball Tower and down the stairs to the Smith Fieldhouse. Tad listened intently and asked very few questions as I recounted the events of 1868. We walked past the tennis courts and I'd nearly wrapped up the story as we got back to the car. Tad warmed up the engine and got the heater going, and I told him about my kiss with David. I rushed through the part about being rescued by Officer Cobb, then waited quietly for Tad's response. I looked at him closely, surprised to see he was very upset.

"Are you saying the only guy you've ever kissed besides me is some old ancestor of mine? That's really bizarre, Emma."

"I know it's bizarre, but it's true!"

He searched my eyes, then shook his head. "Why did you make up this story? Is it a test of my love for you?"

"No, I just want you to know what I've been through," I said. "It's part of your life, too!"

He only laughed. "What an imagination you must have to create such an amazing tale. It's only been four hours since you looked through those genealogy books with Grandpa Charles!"

His words stung deeply. I stared at him, suddenly repulsed that I'd considered marrying him. "Why would I make this up?" I asked.

"I have no idea," he said. "Do you have any proof it happened?"

"Some very firm proof is that my parents and I discovered hundreds of family names based on what Esther told me in Denver, including the names for which you baptized me in the temple! I'm not mentioned in any histories, if that's what you mean. I was only there for a few months. But what about David's statement about love slipping through his fingers? That was about me!"

Tad let out a mocking hoot. "See what I mean? What an

imagination! You really had me believing you for a while." He leaned over to give me a kiss, but I leaned back and slapped him across the face!

"I'll call my parents from the restaurant," I said. "See you around!" In my haste to leave, I stumbled out the door, falling to my knees. As I stood up, Tad said, "The only part of the story that makes sense is your endless clumsiness!"

I was furious now, and realizing I was wearing his engagement ring, I pulled it off my finger and threw it at him, hitting him in the chest. Then I slammed the door and stalked off to the restaurant. Tad sat in his car and watched me go in, and I noticed he stayed there for the next 20 minutes until Dad arrived to pick me up. Once my father arrived, Tad slowly drove away.

I was an emotional wreck, and I cried all the way home. Dad was very concerned, and he finally asked, "Did Tad hurt you?"

"No, he asked me to marry him!"

"And that caused you to burst into tears? I thought you loved him."

"I do, but I told him about my journey, and he didn't believe me!" Then I started wailing again, and Dad wisely kept quiet until we got home. We went into the kitchen, and I calmed down enough to tell my parents what had happened that night. I got a bit angry when smiles occasionally crept across their faces. "Why are you laughing?" I cried. "My life is ruined! Tad will tell everyone now."

"I doubt he'll tell anybody," Dad said. "He loves you, and he'll think about what you've told him. You gave him a lot to ponder without any warning. It's quite a story, especially when it's told to you by the girl you just asked to marry you."

I buried my head into Mom's shoulder, crying for a few minutes, and I began to feel a little better. I even considered calling Tad to patch things up, but then I decided a good night's sleep might clear my head and calm me down.

Chapter Twenty-one

So much for sleeping off my troubles! I awoke irritated and anxious, wanting to call Tad and work things out, but I decided he needed to make the first move. I knew I might be in for a long wait.

I somehow dragged myself to school that morning, and I sat comatose through my first two classes. I usually met Tad at the CougarEat for lunch, but I decided to hide on the fifth floor of the library, where I read a newspaper and nibbled on a bad vending machine sandwich I'd smuggled in. I hated to go to biology, knowing Tad would be there, but I was barely passing the class. I entered the room and saw Tad at the front talking with the instructor. How could he be thinking about an assignment during such a major crisis? He obviously wasn't taking our breakup hard enough!

I took a seat in the back of the room. Tad finally glanced at me, but he didn't give any sign of recognition. Then he sat in the front row. This was our first real quarrel, and I didn't like these mind games one bit! I could only take about 10 minutes of staring at the back of Tad's head before I walked out of the building and spent the rest of the day curled up in my bed. I'd been engaged to Tad for about 20 minutes, and now I'd die a spinster. Life suddenly seemed hopeless.

I stayed in this terrible funk for the next five days, although I did manage to make it to every class except biology. I figured that if Tad and I got together again, he'd help me catch up on my homework. If not, I'd just take an incomplete and retake biology next semester. That's a terrible attitude, but I was now more scatterbrained than usual. For example, I slowly drove past Tad's apartment about four times a day. I think his roommates saw me a few times. I realize now how desperate and pathetic I looked.

My parents were getting worried about my bad attitude and

lack of motivation, so they suggested I start working at Hogi Yogi again, rather than mope around the house all night. I agreed, and I started work the next day. Within a few minutes I was actually smiling at customers and feeling alive for the first time in days. It is amazing how saying, "Do you want hot peppers on that?" dozens of times a night dulls your mind enough to bring a sense of contentment. Between my classes at BYU during the day and working the evening shift at Hogi Yogi, I was too busy to think much about Tad. When another week passed without word from him, our relationship seemed doomed. Our being together had seemed meant to be, but not all fairy tales come true.

One night after work Mom greeted me with a casual smile. "Dad and Doug are playing Yahtzee if you want to join them."

"No thanks," I said. "I've got some homework to do."

"That reminds me. Tad brought you some biology homework. He said he'd come back at ten o'clock."

My head jerked up to look at the clock. It was five minutes to ten. I sprinted to my room, ignoring Mom's laughter, and ripped off my Hogi Yogi uniform. I pulled on a sweater and jeans and touched up my makeup. I convinced myself Tad had come over because he was too nice to let me throw away my biology grade. He probably just wanted to patch things up so we could be "friends." I could live with that, since I'd surely fail biology without him.

Within seconds the doorbell rang, and as Mom let Tad in the door, I slipped into the kitchen. "Hello, Tad," Mom said sweetly. "Come take a seat on the couch. I'll get Emma."

I heard him move to the couch, and Mom entered the kitchen with a smirk on her face. "Go out there and get your boyfriend back!" she whispered. "The poor boy is shaking like a leaf."

I stepped into the room, and Tad gave me a nervous smile. "It's so good to see you!" he said. "I've really missed our lunches together."

"And I've really missed biology," I said. We both laughed,

knowing it was a blatant lie. Maybe becoming friends again would work out. I wasn't giving into his charms too easily, though, and I took a seat at the other end of the couch.

"Don't worry, I'll help you catch up on your homework," he said.

"Oh, are we going to be spending time together?" I asked. "If I recall correctly, I'm still waiting for an apology."

He slapped his hand to his forehead. "Have a little patience," he said. "I'm getting to it!"

We heard Mom snicker from around the corner, and we went silent. Then she said, "All right, I'll go to my room!"

We listened to her walk away, then Tad said, "Emma, I'm so sorry! I believe your story."

"That's quite a change of heart," I said, not quite ready to believe him.

"I was willing to believe anything, as long as you'd still love me. I went over the story a dozen times in my head, and I was finally convinced it could've possibly happened."

"Possibly? It did, Tad!"

"I know that now. I finally went to visit Grandpa Charles, and I told him the story…"

"You told him? How dare you!"

"Don't worry, he's the only person I've told!" he said, cutting off my next question.

"Grandpa found your experience to be very interesting, and he told me to wait while he searched for something in the basement. He returned with a dusty folder that held an old hand-written journal. Grandpa said he didn't think anyone had even looked at the journal in several years. I asked him what it was, and as he blew the dust off the cover, he said, 'It's the life history of David North.'"

Tad paused to reach around the couch. He pulled out a book with a faded brown cover. I hardly dared hope what it contained! Tad opened to a spot near the end of the book, then handed the book to me. "I've been reading through this thing for three straight days," he said with a tired grin. "I nearly gave up, but I finally found something you might enjoy."

I looked down at the journal and began reading. It read:

August 11, 1921

With the recent passing of my beloved Judy, I've been thinking a lot about the events of my life. There's one episode I've kept in my heart and rarely mentioned for fear of hurting Judy's feelings, but I doubt she'll mind now if I jot it down. It was quite an adventure, and I want my grandchildren to know I visited Denver when it was the size of Heber, and I survived many things on that trip, such as getting beat up by gold thieves and having my horse stolen at gunpoint by Indians.

These events took place when I was 19, in the summer of 1868, and they happened because of a beautiful young woman named Emma Dalton. She came in and out of my life like a brief flash of wonderful sunlight. I've never met another girl like her, except for my lovely Judy, of course.

Tears came to my eyes, and Tad started crying, too. I leaned toward him and kissed him long and hard. Then I resumed reading David's description of our journey. The whole story was there, although David claimed I caused most of the mishaps! I guess he was right. David wasn't sure how I had disappeared, but he thought I'd run out the back of the barn and headed down Provo Canyon.

He wrote that the Daltons weren't surprised I'd vanished, so a search for me was never organized. David mentioned he'd traveled to Springville in early 1869 to locate me, and while the Johnson family remembered me, they hadn't seen me in nearly a year, so David had given up his search.

I closed the book and scooted close to Tad. "Thank you for believing me," I said. "You mean everything to me."

"You're welcome," he said. "I'm sorry I ever doubted you."

He searched for something in his shirt pocket. "I've been hoping you'd like to wear this again," he said, holding up the engagement ring.

"I'd love to! I've regretted ever taking it off." I slipped the ring on my finger. Then I hugged Tad tightly, never wanting to let go.

Chapter Twenty-two

Tad and I didn't immediately set a wedding date, but we agreed to be married July 20th after I made a visit to my neighbor Beth Jensen. She had called me a few days after we'd announced our engagement, and she said it was urgent I visit her. I told her I'd come over the next afternoon.

When I went to her house, I noticed an unfamiliar car in the driveway. I knocked, and Beth let me in. She introduced me to an elderly woman named Maggie Chappell. Beth explained that Maggie had been a childhood friend. We chatted a moment about the nice spring weather. Then the two of them sat on the couch while I took a seat in an easychair. "Beth, I'm sorry I never came to help you with the flowerbeds," I said.

"That's fine, Emma. You've been busier these past few months than we could've imagined," she said. "Besides, your mother says you have even bigger plans coming up. May we see your engagement ring?"

I held my hand toward the ladies, and they "oohed" and "aahed" appropriately. It wasn't a fancy ring, but I loved its design with a center diamond surrounded by three smaller diamonds.

"It's beautiful," Maggie said. "Seeing your ring reminds me of what Beth and I would like to talk to you about."

Beth shifted nervously on the couch. "Since you were closer to Leah than anyone, what we're about to say should make complete sense to you."

"When it comes to Leah, I have a tender spot in my heart," I said. "She was my dear friend, and I hope she's happy in the spirit world."

Maggie cleared her throat and said, "Speaking of that, I think Leah wants be even happier over there. I am Harold Milton's sister, by the way."

She paused to let that sink in. The name Harold Milton came rushing back. He was Leah's "soldier boy," the one who had died in World War II!

"What are you saying?" I asked.

"Well, Beth and I haven't seen each other in years, and I didn't even know Leah had died. I live in Ogden and rarely come to Springville anymore, but lately I've had a nagging feeling that Harold is impatient about something. I'm his little sister, and when we were younger, if I whined about a chore, he'd say, 'Don't dwell on it, just do it!' The past few days that phrase has come into my mind many times, and I know he's trying to tell me something. I felt impressed to call Beth, and she's been having the same type of promptings with regard to Leah."

Beth nodded. "I think Leah is trying to make sure I get the message," she said. "It's becoming clear those two lovebirds want to be sealed for eternity! Their sealing surely would've happened in this life if Harold had survived, and Leah always regretted she hadn't been sealed to him when she'd had the chance. Now that they're both in the spirit world, I don't think they want to wait around any longer."

As the women spoke, I felt tingles shoot through my entire body. I knew they were speaking the truth! "Can it be done?" I asked.

"I've talked to the stake president, and he said that in special cases, sealings have been performed for worthy engaged couples when one or both unexpectedly die before marriage. Of course, the consent of both families is required," Beth said. "I feel it's right, and so does Maggie. We're Harold and Leah's only living siblings, so family consent isn't a problem. The stake president says we should wait a year after Leah's death, but he has talked with the proper authorities, and they've given full approval."

Those tingles came rushing back again. I jumped to my feet and said, "That's wonderful! Leah will be so happy! Who will represent them during the sealing?"

Beth and Maggie watched me steadily. Then Beth said, "Nothing would make Leah happier than if you and Tad represented them in the temple."

I was overwhelmed! Through tears of joy, I agreed to take part. They stood, and we held each other tightly. As we hugged, the spiritual feeling in the room became overpowering, and I feel Leah had joined us to share her excitement. I was also pleased for another reason. It appeared that Beth, known so unkindly as "Sister Ice" during her teaching years, had finally experienced a warming of the heart.

I'd often talked to Tad about Leah, so he knew all about her, and he's excited and honored to take part in their sealing ordinance. So on July 20th, we'll be part of a double wedding. Tad and I will first be sealed for time and all eternity in the Provo Temple. Then immediately following our ceremony, we will be sealed in behalf of Harold Milton and Leah Jensen. I expect there will be wedding receptions on both sides of the veil that night!

So Leah was right. I had a mission to perform, and although I came awfully close, I completed it without getting killed! Tad says he isn't taking anything for granted, though. He half-jokingly says he expects the sealing ceremony to be delayed indefinitely when I stumble and hit my head on the altar! If that occurs, I hope to stay in the same time zone, but stranger things have happened!

So that's how the last year of my life has gone. People have told me the first year of marriage is full of hectic new experiences, but I hope the coming year is more peaceful than the last year has been. I was hesitant to share my story, but I finally have because it shows how the Lord can use even a clumsy, average girl to move His kingdom forward. I have no doubt you're more talented than I am, and I know the Lord is eager to use your talents, if you'll just let Him.

We all have an Esther Sheridan, and yes, even a hot-tempered Henry eagerly waiting for us to track them down. As we search out their records and perform temple ordinances for them, our family on both sides of the veil is blessed.

Trust in the Lord, and He'll guide you to the answers you seek. And if you get the urge to search out some of your own crazy ancestors, go for it! Perhaps you'll find yourself on a wild adventure of your own. Good luck, and watch your step!

About the Author

Chad G. Daybell lives in Springville, Utah, with his wife, Tammy, and their four children. He graduated from BYU with a bachelor's degree in Journalism, where he served as *The Daily Universe's* city editor. He spent three years as a copy editor at *The Standard-Examiner* in Ogden, Utah, before accepting employment in Springville. He served an LDS mission among the Spanish-speaking people of New Jersey. He enjoys hiking with his sons, and dancing with his wife and daughters.